THE BUCKET LIST

RACHEL HANNA

PROLOGUE

*M*y hand grips my phone, as it does around this time each day, while I stare at the GPS app. Watching my *technically* adult daughter make the one hour drive from her workplace to her apartment always puts me on edge. It's not that I don't trust her. I do. I just don't trust every single other idiotic individual on the road next to her.

I sit on my patio like this every evening, having my cup of decaf coffee, staring at her car moving. Well, it's not really her car. It's a little blue dot. And sometimes, when it sits for too long, I panic. I think all kinds of scary thoughts like what if she crashed and needs my help? It's not like I own a pair of those "jaws of life", but doesn't everybody need their mom when they're scared?

Oh gosh, what if she's scared? What if she's sitting there with her hazard lights on in the middle of that busy Atlanta interstate, cars whizzing by, and nobody is stopping to help her? What if she's having an asthma attack? Wait, does she still carry that rescue inhaler I got her before she went off to college almost four years ago? Is it expired? Oh, geez, what kind of mother sends her kid off with an expired inhaler?

The little dot starts moving again, and I let out the breath I've been holding. As soon as Annie makes it home, I'm calling the pharmacy to make sure she has a new inhaler.

Even though she moved out years ago to go to college, I still can't shake the feeling that something bad is going to happen to her. After all, it's not without precedence. Her father died right in front of me when she was seven years old, and I've never gotten over the feeling that I need to watch after her even more carefully.

I don't like to think about the day Jesse died. He was the love of my life, and I still haven't dated. Yeah, it's been fifteen years, and I haven't joined any of those dating apps or gone to a singles bar. Jesse set the bar too high for any other man to reach.

Why is it, when someone you love dies, they suddenly have no faults? I can't think of one fault that man had, but I know he had some because we were in marriage counseling when he died. Those bad memories have been wiped out of my brain. I only remember positive things. I guess that's a good thing, but it sure has made the last fifteen years lonely.

Just as I'm allowing myself to go down a mental rabbit hole, my phone rings, scaring the absolute crap out of me. I hope it's not Annie because that would either mean she's driving and using her phone (which is a major no-no), or she's in trouble.

Instead, I see that it's my best friend in the whole world, Monica. She's always a light on a dark day. She's been there for every single life event I've had since we were both ten years old, when I showed up at our elementary school as the new kid. I had unwieldy curly brown hair and an enormous gap between my front teeth that you could've stuck two quarters through, but she liked me anyway. I will never understand why.

"Hello?"

"Hey, Jilly!" She has always called me Jilly. She knows I hate it. She does not care one iota.

"Hey, Mon. What's up?"

"Oh, just sitting here eating a big bowl of cereal and looking at the ocean." Typical Monica. Eating cereal instead of a proper dinner. It probably has those little colored marshmallows in it.

Monica is what one would call "lucky". She lives in a beautiful home sitting right on the ocean in Pawley's Island, South Carolina. Her ex-husband, who she was married to for about sixteen months many moons ago, gave it to her in the divorce. Monica is lucky like that. Everyone likes her, and they always have. Even her ex-husband likes her. Of course, they've been divorced for over ten years now. The place is paid off and probably worth a fortune.

Monica is successful in her own right, too. She sells real estate when she wants to, and it's always these multi-million dollar homes. When she gets a commission check, it's more than I make in a year.

She lives alone and loves it. Monica never had kids of her own. Just didn't want them. Thinks of Annie as her child, too. Instead, Monica has traveled the world and gone on so many adventures that I can't even keep count. Bali, Thailand, some little village in Peru. She's been to places I didn't even know existed.

Now, I would never want to do the things she does. The thought of getting on an airplane alone and going across the world does not appeal to me in the slightest. But I'm glad she's happy. She comes home and shows me pictures. Tells me stories. That is more than enough for me.

"Are you ever going to grow up and eat actual food?"

"Like what?"

"Broccoli? Spinach?"

Monica makes a gagging sound. "That sounds horrible. I did eat alligator once. Didn't care for it."

"Yuck."

"Come on! You know I'm an adventurous eater."

"The most adventurous I get is putting too much salt on my mashed potatoes."

Monica laughs. "Oh, you wild woman."

"So, how did your day go?"

She pauses for a long moment. "Not great, but let's not talk about that. How's Annie?"

I look down at the GPS app and notice she's made it back to her apartment. "She made it home."

"Are you still watching that GPS app every day?"

"Of course."

"You realize that's not normal, right? She's twenty-two years old, Jilly. You have to let her fly."

"She can fly, but I can watch her while she does it."

I hear her chuckle under her breath. "You can't protect everyone from everything." This is something she tells me often, but I never really listen. If I'd been paying better attention to my late husband, he might still be with me today. We would've celebrated twenty-five years of marriage this year. Instead, I hid under the covers and cried on the fifteenth anniversary of his death.

"I can try."

"Honey, you'll drive yourself crazy living like this. You need to get out there, meet people, maybe meet a nice man. Fall in love. Get a dog."

"I'm happy like I am."

"No, you're not. You deserve fun, Jilly. And love. Lots and lots of love."

"Why are you talking like this?"

Monica sighs. "I guess I just miss my best friend. Any chance you can drive up tomorrow?"

"Tomorrow? That's kind of short notice, don't you think?" Monica lives on Pawley's Island, but I live about an hour and a half away inland. It's a nice enough area, but I'd much rather be on the beach like she is. What a gift it must be to wake up every day and see the ocean. It's my favorite place on earth.

It's not like I can't make the trip. After all, it's my weekend off from the restaurant, and I have nothing else to do except laundry. Who wants to spend the weekend staring at their dirty underwear while it spins round and round?

"Come on. I've been feeling a little blue. I need you to come drink wine and judge people wearing horrible swimsuits with me."

I laugh. When Monica and I are together, we're like two hyper-critical fashion correspondents, although neither of us has a clue how to dress ourselves. I spend all my off time in yoga pants and t-shirts, although I haven't done yoga a day in my life. Monica wears beach clothes and jumpsuits like it's her job.

"Okay, fine. But you're buying me lunch at that taco place."

Monica laughs. "Always with the taco place. You know, we have other places to eat here."

"Why change to something else when I know I like the taco place?"

She sighs. "Oh, Jilly. You're like an old lady in an almost fifty-year-old's body."

I GET to Pawley's Island a lot earlier than I planned, but it will give me a chance to surprise Monica. We haven't seen each other face-to-face in over three months. The restaurant, which I manage now, is always so busy. It's a country kitchen with things like biscuits and gravy, meatloaf, and fried catfish, and locals love it. I hate working there, but one has to make ends meet, I suppose.

I walk up the steep front steps of Monica's beach house. It's painted this beautiful aqua color that sounds tacky, but fits right in with the other houses on the street. It sits up on stilts, and I can see Monica's little sports car parked underneath, right next to that ping-pong table she never uses, and the kayak she insisted on buying two years ago. I won't get in the thing because I saw this story on the news once where a woman died when her kayak flipped, and she got trapped underneath it.

There's also a car I don't recognize in the driveway. She must've bought yet another vehicle she doesn't need. It's cute, but I like big vehicles. More protection on the road from crazy drivers.

I look through the glass door and don't see her, so I knock. She doesn't have a doorbell. Who doesn't have a doorbell on a house worth over a million dollars? After waiting a few minutes, I get worried, so I dig into my purse and find the extra key she gave me years ago.

I turn the key and step into the house, which has beautiful white tile floors throughout. I like carpet myself, but that doesn't exactly work when you live on the beach.

"Mon?" The house is quiet, and she's not answering me. "You're scaring me, Mon. Where are you?"

Just as I'm about to call the police - because I've been known to panic quickly - I hear her voice. It's faint, but I hear it. I walk straight through the living room and see her sitting outside on the deck. She's wearing her fluffy white robe, and there's a woman standing next to her. I step closer, trying to be the super spy that I'm not.

There's a tall silver pole, and then I realize it's an IV pole like the ones at the hospital. There's a bag attached with some liquid in it. Maybe one of those fancy Vitamin C drips rich people get done at home? She's never mentioned it to me, though.

She looks tired with her head leaned back and her face toward the sky. Is she asleep? I couldn't sleep with a needle in my arm.

I quietly push the door open a bit further to try to hear their conversation. It's hard with waves rolling in just beyond her deck and walkway.

"How long have you been best friends?" the woman asks.

"Almost forty years now. Hard to believe."

"Why haven't you told her?" *Told me what?*

"I just haven't known how. She doesn't handle stress well."

"Monica, you need to tell her today."

"Well, I kind of have to. I don't want her to be blindsided."

My stomach clenches, so I step back and take a deep breath. There's bad news coming. I hate getting bad news. I'd rather her just blurt it out than keep me in suspense. I won't even watch suspenseful movies. I hate knowing something shocking is coming. Give me romantic comedy movies all day long.

"Okay, we're all done for today. Remember to drink as much water as you can tolerate." The woman starts removing the IV, so I run like a scared cat back through the front door and onto the porch. A few moments later, I see her walk around the side of the house and get into her car, pulling past mine down the short driveway. I knock on the door like I just got there.

Monica makes her way to the front door and forces a smile. She's still wearing her robe.

"Jilly, you're a good half hour early."

"You know me!" I say, trying desperately not to cry as I wait for this news she needs to tell me.

"Come on in," she says, sounding a little tired. Maybe the early morning sunshine took it out of her while she sat on the deck.

She leads me into the living room, and we sit down on her fluffy white sofa. Everything she owns is fluffy and white. At my house, I have a lot of colors that don't necessarily go together. A red floral sofa handed down to me sixteen years ago. An over-sized tan arm chair I found at a thrift store. Years of stuff cobbled together to make a home.

Monica sits at one end, and I sit at the other. We face each other, pulling our legs up underneath us. We've sat this way since we were kids. The ocean splays out behind Monica's head in the gigantic windows that bring in so much light.

"Still in your robe, huh?" I say, trying to make light of it.

She looks down. "Oh, yeah. I got a late start this morning."

"Mon, what's really going on?" I can't hold it in. I have no "chill", as my daughter says.

"What do you mean?"

"Who was that woman who just left?"

Her face falls a bit. She looks pale this morning. Normally, Monica is tan, and her skin is full of life. She looks way younger than our age, but not today.

"What woman? Did you add alcohol to your decaf coffee this morning?" She makes fun of me for drinking decaf, but if I don't I get panic attacks from the caffeine. I wouldn't have been a good drug addict if caffeine affects me so strongly.

"I let myself in because I got here early. I heard you talking, and I saw the IV. Now, let's have an actual conversation, okay?"

She stares at me in a way I haven't seen before. Just looks at me like she's run into a brick wall. For a moment I worry she's having one of those seizures that don't look like seizures. I saw a story about those on the news. Scary stuff.

"Jilly, I have cancer, and it's not good, sweetie."

"What? No, that's not possible. You're the health-iest person I know! You drink all that seagrass…"

"Wheatgrass," she says, laughing softly.

"What kind is it?"

"The bad kind," she says, chuckling.

"It's not funny, Mon."

"I'm okay with it, Jilly."

"The doctor must be wrong…"

"I've gotten three opinions, and I've had every test known to man. I ignored some symptoms I shouldn't have, and it came back to bite me."

"So that was chemo you were doing?"

She shook her head. "No, that was a vitamin cocktail, and some nausea medicine."

"You needed that because of the chemo?"

She paused a moment and then cleared her throat. "I declined chemo, Jilly."

I stand up. "What? Why on earth would you do a thing like that?"

"Because I weighed the options. Have chemo and get a few more months of a miserable life, or go out the way I want to."

"Wait. Go out? What does that mean?" I sit back down, afraid my legs won't hold me.

"Honey, you know what that means. This is my last adventure."

"No. This isn't happening."

She scoots closer and puts her hand on my arm. "I don't have much longer, Jilly."

"Why didn't you tell me?"

"Because I spent the first few weeks doing all

kinds of adventures, trying to make the most of my time. Then I got too tired and weak. I had to come home, and I wanted to see you one more time."

"One more time? Surely it's not that... quick?"

She nods, her eyes filling with tears. "Hospice is coming next week, Jilly. They're going to make me comfortable."

"No, that can't be right. Please start chemo, Monica. Try something! Anything!"

"None of it will work, and it will just make me miserable. I've had a glorious life. You know that. I can't wait to see what's on the other side. I just worry about you."

"Me? Why?"

"Well, you've always leaned on me, and I hate leaving you. We're a team."

I smile sadly as tears roll down my cheeks. "I can't do this life without you."

"Sure, you can. Jill, you're stronger than you know."

"I'm really not," I say, full-on crying now. We fall into each other's arms and sob.

"Promise me something," she says, her face pressed into my shoulder.

"What?"

"What ever I ask of you in my will, you'll do it."

I pull back and look at her. "I'd do anything for you, Mon."

She smiles. "Good. That gives me some peace."

We hug for what seems like years before breaking apart. The hug will never be long enough.

CHAPTER 1

I can't believe it's been two weeks since my best friend died. Even after hospice came to take care of her, she lasted another three weeks. She was strong and feisty and always proving everyone wrong.

I thought she might beat it. If anyone could, it would've been Monica. But cancer won… again.

"You about ready?"

The only saving grace of this whole situation is Annie. She came home as soon as the school session was over, and she stayed with me. We went back to see Monica one more time, while she could still sit and talk with us. She was weak then, and very thin. Thinner than when she went on that weird cabbage diet in college.

Monica's memorial service was small. She kept her circle tight, so it was just a few family members, me, and Annie. Her ex-husband came too, and he sobbed like a baby when he saw her urn. She wanted to be cremated. I haven't thought about what I want when I die, mainly because I'm terrified to think of such things.

"I just need to put on my lipstick." The wildest thing I do each day is put on red lipstick. My husband loved it, so I still do it. Weird, I know, but it's a part of me now.

Today is the reading of Monica's will. It still sounds so weird to say things like that. She would've turned fifty in seven months. Six weeks after that, I will turn fifty. That makes me feel old, especially without Monica here.

I was thankful that I got Monica's ashes. Her mother died years ago, and her aunt didn't want them. She wasn't exactly close to her family, but at least they came.

I pick up the ashes, which are housed in a chic and shiny silver urn, and walk toward the door.

"You're bringing the ashes?" Annie asks, her nose scrunched up.

"It's your Aunt Monica, not ashes from the fireplace."

I don't give her a chance to respond, and instead grab my ugly black purse and walk out into the garage. Monica bought purses as often as she bought toilet paper. She loved them. The purses, not the toilet paper.

We get into my older compact car and pull out of the one-car garage attached to my condo. It's a nice enough place, especially for someone who manages a restaurant. After being at Monica's beach house so much, I realize just how little space I have. Plus, her deck overlooked the ocean. My tiny slab patio over-looks Mrs. Ellison's backyard of weeds and plastic lawn chairs she's thrown out like they will recycle themselves.

"How are you feeling, Momma?"

I shrug my shoulders. "Empty. Stunned. A little hungry."

She smiles slightly. "You and Aunt Monica always used humor in sad situations."

"She did it more than I did, but I'm trying to pick up the banner and run with it."

We drive in silence, except for the radio playing seventies hits in the background, for the ten-minute drive to the attorney's office. Thankfully, Monica had her will done with an attorney local to me to make things easier. She always took care of me, even from afar.

It's weird how I still feel her near me, even without the ashes. I brought them along because it only seems fair she is at her will reading. It is *her* will, after all.

"What do you think she said in her will?" Annie asks me after a few minutes.

"I think she'll leave the house to her ex-husband, and that makes sense. He bought it in the first place. I think she may leave you some money for your college loans. Aside from that, she'll probably leave me her collection of expensive handbags because she always hated my cheap ones."

"I can't say I blame her on that one. Seriously, can you ditch that old thing?" She nods her head in the direction of the backseat where my beloved black purse sits, not bothering a soul.

"Hey, that purse has been with me through it all. It's comfortable and broken in."

"I wish someone would break in and take it."

I laugh, despite my grief. Sometimes, it feels weird to laugh. My best friend died. I don't think I'm supposed to laugh again. Besides, she was always the one who made me laugh.

The day she died, I was holding her hand. I

hope she knew I was there. I think she did. While she passed, we opened all the windows so she could feel the ocean breeze and hear the waves one last time. It was the most peaceful passing I could imagine.

"Okay, we're here." I put the car in park and reach back for my ugly handbag. Annie carefully picks up the urn. I keep trying to explain the top won't just fall off like a cookie jar, but she remains very careful like she's holding a bomb.

"Here," she says, handing it to me when we meet in front of the car. "I love her, but carrying her ashes around is just creepy, Mom."

To some extent, I don't think I'm actually handling her death well. I went straight back to work, and didn't give myself a grieving period at all. It feels like if I stop and grieve for even a moment, I may never get up off the floor.

We walk into the nondescript building on Main Street. It's near the town square, and it's just white with a small front porch. Lawyers seem to love buying old houses and making them offices in literally every town in America.

"Can I help you?" The woman in the little window is older. Okay, she looks ancient. Like maybe when time began, God chipped her out of a stone. Maybe I am a little more ornery than usual this morning.

"We're here for a will reading..." I say.

"Oh, yes. For Monica Dayton? How terrible to pass so young." She stares at me waiting for some kind of response, but I have none. Just check me in, lady. I don't need your commentary on my friend dying. Once she realizes I'm not responding, she clears her throat and looks down at a paper. "Please, have a seat. Dan will be with you shortly."

Dan is the attorney handing Monica's estate. It feels weird to think that. *Monica's estate*. Do I have an estate? Not unless you count my ratty old sofa and a bunch of clothes that don't fit anymore.

"This place smells funny," Annie says when we sit down.

"It's old and musty."

She leans closer. "Like that lady?"

I bump her with my shoulder. "Annie! Not nice." Of course, she gets her dark sense of humor from me. I use humor for everything. It covers a lot.

"Jill Rogers?" A man opens a creaky door and calls my name. He's tall, lanky, and wearing little glasses that barely cover his eyes. His hair is slightly too long for his age, almost touching his shoulders. He's wearing a Hawaiian shirt and a pair of khaki shorts, along with some boat shoes that have seen better days. Who is this clown?

"That's me," I say standing up. Annie joins me.

"I'm Dan Archer. Come on back." He holds the door open, and Annie and I cross in front of him. He smells of way too much cologne, and I struggle not to sneeze. My sense of smell is way too sharp. Monica used to say I should get a job as one of those dogs who looks for missing people and dead bodies.

We wait in the hallway until Dan leads us to his office. It's just as one would imagine - big mahogany desk, a wall of books on custom, built-in book-shelves. I wasn't expecting the enormous collection of superhero figurines on the other side of the room. There must be thousands of dollars there.

"Comic book fan?" I ask.

He grins from ear to ear. "Big time."

I make the mistake of looking at my daughter, who mouths, "nerd".

"That's quite a collection."

He looks over at the shelving unit across the room with pride on his face. "I've been collecting since I was eight years old. Anyway, you didn't come here to talk about my inability to grow up. You came to discuss Monica's will."

I look around. "Shouldn't we wait on the others?"

He looks perplexed. "What others?"

My eyes widen. "Wait. You mean we're the only beneficiaries?"

"Yep." He stares at me, slightly smiling. I want to ask him if he realizes I don't consider this to be like a lottery win. My best friend died, and I'd rather have her back than all the money in the world. I refrain.

"How can that be? Monica had an ex-husband who was still a dear friend to her. She had a wide circle of friends."

"Mom, let the man talk," Annie chides, giving me that look that always makes me want to pinch her arm.

"It's okay. I'm sure this has been a shocking, upsetting time," he says, before picking up the file on his desk. He opens it to reveal a small thumb drive and a few pieces of what look to be legal paperwork.

"What's that?" I point to the drive just as he plugs it into his laptop and turns the screen around. Monica's face lights up the screen. This video was obviously taken weeks, or even months ago. She still looks like Monica and not the shell of the human she looked like when she passed.

"Monica wanted to explain her decisions to you on video. Shall I press play?"

"Of course." I hug her urn closer to me, and I'm

thankful he hasn't mentioned that Monica is "here" with us. He just ignores the fact that she's sitting in my lap.

He presses the button on his computer, and suddenly the room is filled with the voice of my best friend. A peace comes over me, but it's short-lived when I feel the cold metal of her urn on my arms.

"Hey, Jilly," she starts. Even in death she's calling me that, knowing good and well I can't do a dang thing about it. *"I hope Annie is there, too. If so, hey, Annie Bell!"* She always called Annie that. I don't think she minds.

"So, it turns out I'm dead. That stinks, right?" I giggle slightly. She always made me laugh so hard. *"I know you're struggling. I didn't want to leave you. We were supposed to hit our fifties hard, but now I can't be there to make you do the things I was going to make you do. Jump out of an airplane, go white water rafting..."*

"She was never going to convince me to do those things," I say, leaning over to Annie.

"Shhh," she says, again making me want to pinch her.

"What you don't know is that I started a blog a couple of years ago."

"A blog? She never told me that," I mutter. I'm a little miffed that she kept it from me.

"The blog follows my adventures. I posted videos of my last trip to Bali, that volcano excursion in Guatemala... well, a bunch of things. I kept it from you because you always think I'm doing dangerous stuff, and you worry I'll end up dead. Well, I guess that ship has sailed..."

"Such a bad joke," Annie says, shaking her head.

"Shhh," I say, getting her back for shushing me earlier.

"My biggest worry about leaving you is that you'll never truly live, Jilly. You don't have to do crazy stuff like me, although it always makes me feel so alive. But you don't live. You're doing a job you hate. You're constantly watching that silly GPS app, wondering if Annie made it from her apartment to the grocery store..."

Dan gives me a sideways look, but then goes back to looking at the screen. Did Dan just judge me for worrying about my daughter's safety on the dangerous roads?

"So, I have a proposition for you. First, I'm paying off Annie's college loans no matter what, so she can rest easy for the rest of this video."

Annie smiles and leans back in her chair. She looks over at the urn. "Thanks, Aunt Monica."

"But you have a bigger hill to climb, my best friend. I'm going to leave everything I own to you. All my bank accounts. My beach house. My car. Everything."

My mouth drops open, and Annie stares at me, stifling a smile. "She left you everything?"

"You just can't have it until you complete some tasks for me. And, you have to prove you've completed said tasks to my blog followers. My attorney has instructions to post my obituary there, along with the instructions I'm about to give you. He also has the login information for you."

"What on earth?" I stammer as she continues talking.

"I was supposed to turn fifty soon, and it's likely I didn't make it. I need you to complete my bucket list, Jilly. It's just a few things, but I won't rest easy until I know they're done."

"Absolutely not!"

"As long as you complete everything by what would've been my birthday, you get it all. I know right now you're thinking I'm being harsh, but I'm so worried about you. I want you to have fun. Have love. I know you'll sink further away from both things if I don't have you go out into the world and actually live. This is done in love."

"Obviously, she had lost her mind at this point," I say out loud to no one in particular.

"Each time you complete something, you must take photos and write a blog post. My attorney will watch, and he can check them off the list. Each task is in a separate

envelope that my attorney will give you. I've allowed for a budget so you can take time off work, or better yet quit that dead-end job, and focus solely on completing my list."

Dan waves a stack of ivory colored envelopes in my direction.

"I know the big question is what happens if you refuse to do this, or you don't finish everything? I mean, there has to be a penalty, right? The beach house will go to my ex, and you'll only get ten percent of what's in my bank accounts. Oh, and you can have my purses, because God knows you need a new purse."

"True story," Annie says as she stares down at her phone.

"Please do this, Jilly. Live for me. Live for yourself. Make this next stage of your life the best yet. Go live double now, for both of us. I'll be on the other side, cheering you on. I know we'll meet again, and when we do, I want to hear about all of your adventures. I want to hear that you fell madly in love with a wonderful man. I want only the very best for you, even if you don't think so right now. I have to go now. I love you and Annie. You were and always will be my family. Be brave, Jilly girl. I love you so much."

I can barely see the screen through my hot tears. I stand up quickly and rush toward the door, down the hall, and out onto the sidewalk, my breath quicker than I've ever felt it. I bend over, trying to get more air. I'm sure people on the street are looking at me like I'm a lunatic.

"Mom, are you okay?" I feel Annie's hand on my upper back.

I continue sucking air, like there's not enough in the world around me. "Why would she do this to me?" I finally eke out.

"She loved you. She wanted you to have adventures like she did."

I'm finally able to catch my breath and stand upright. "I don't like adventures."

Annie chuckles. "Yeah, we all know that. Aunt Monica just wanted you to have a full life, and I guess in the end she decided to force you to do it."

"Well, I'm not doing it," I say, shaking my head.

"Mom, you have to do it! It was her last wish."

"She's just going to have to be mad at me in the afterlife then, because I'm not jumping off a bridge or setting myself on fire or riding the world's most dangerous roller coaster. There's no telling what's on that list!"

"Why don't we at least go open an envelope?"

I consider the thought for a moment. "I guess that would make sense."

Annie opens the door to the office, and we walk

inside. The woman behind the desk is looking at me like I'm a crazy person, and maybe I am. I've had anxiety my whole life, but today's events have taken it to levels I didn't know existed.

When we finally make it into Dan's office, he's still sitting there with a smile on his face. Monica's face is frozen on the screen.

"Sorry about that. I was just a bit… overwhelmed."

"Monica told me you aren't a big risk taker and that this would probably cause quite a bit of anxiety."

I laugh. "Well, she was right about that."

"If it makes you feel any better, she told me these tasks are much less adventurous than what you'd expect. She left these to the end of her bucket list because they were more on the boring side."

Somehow, I know that Monica's idea of boring and my idea of boring are vastly different.

"Can I open an envelope?"

He nods and hands it to me. "Take a look."

I slowly open it, making eye contact with Annie, who is giving me an encouraging look. Of course she wants me to do whatever is on the paper because she wants to visit that beach house as often as she can.

"Read it out loud," Annie says.

I clear my throat and stare at the paper. Monica had obviously lost her mind when she wrote this.

"Take salsa dancing lessons."

"That's not so bad!" Annie says, laughing. "Can she open another one?"

Dan nods and hands it to me.

"Zip line through the trees."

"You can do that."

I snatch several more envelopes off his desk and start opening them like a rabid raccoon.

"Enter a gardening contest?"

"Well, that's kind of a weird one."

"Kiss a stranger? Crash a class reunion? What in the heck are these?"

Dan shrugs his shoulders. "All I can say is that Monica picked these especially for you."

"Is that all of them?" Annie asks.

"No, there are others," Dan says, sliding the stack away from me so I can't open them.

"Mom..."

"Listen, why don't you go home and think it over for a few days? Call me after New Year's and let me know what you decide." He stands up and basically invites us to leave.

I stand up too. "I'll think about it, but this is all

too much. I like my life. I like routine. I always have, and I'm unlikely to change now."

Annie eyes me suspiciously. She knows I'm lying. She knows I don't enjoy my life. I hate when I can't lie because my kid is standing there. All that parental pressure to be a good role model.

"Well, I do hope you'll change your mind. Monica put a lot of thought into this," Dan says, applying pressure like any talented attorney would.

I don't respond and instead just slightly nod my head as I walk toward the door.

"Mom?" Annie calls from behind me.

"What?" I'm miffed that she ruined my perfectly good storming off episode.

"Aunt Monica?" She points to the chair where I've left my best friend's ashes.

I walk over and snatch the urn up. Right now, I'm so aggravated with my best friend, I might just make her ride in the back seat.

CHAPTER 2

*A*fter a strong glass of wine… or three… I go to bed. I dream of Monica as she always was, dancing and laughing, which causes me to wake up with tears running down my face.

Life isn't fair.

I can't fall back asleep, so I climb out of my warm bed and walk toward the kitchen. Maybe a glass of water will magically put me back to sleep. Oh, who am I fooling? I know there are chocolate chip cookies in there. I'm going to eat the cookies. There will be no water involved in this little escapade.

"What are you doing up?" Annie says from the darkness. I jump a good two feet off the floor, which I could never do again if I tried. I'm a little plump these days. I'm still going to eat the cookies.

"Good Lord, child! What are you trying to do? Kill me?"

She laughs. "It's not like I jumped out from behind the breakfast bar with a butcher knife, Mom."

I open the cabinet and retrieve my beloved cookies before pouring a glass of cold milk. I sit at the table across from her, pointing to the cookies. She shakes her head.

"Don't judge me. My best friend died and is now trying to kill me from beyond the grave," I say, before shoving one of the sugar-filled miracles into my mouth. God was really at his best the day he created sugar.

"Are you going to do it?"

"Well, get right to the point, why don't you?"

"I've been up thinking about it all night."

"You just want a beach house," I say, rolling my eyes. "Never mind that I'll probably die in the process."

"Mom, you know Aunt Monica would never make you do something that could kill you."

I stare at her. "Listen, what I think will kill me and what Monica thought would kill me are two different things."

"I'll do some of them with you," she says, grinning at me.

"You're in school. You're going to quit to complete a bucket list with your mother?"

"Well, no, but I can come some weekends when I'm not doing my internship." Annie is in school to be a broadcast journalist, and she's working at a local Atlanta TV station as an intern.

"I appreciate it, honey, but you need to focus on school."

"I know you can do this," she says, reaching over and patting my hand. "And I think in your own terrified, anxious way, you kind of want to."

"I most certainly do not want to."

She stands up and kisses the top of my head. "Aunt Monica wanted the best for you. Do this last thing for her, okay?"

She walks away, and I can hear her pad up the stairs before closing her bedroom door. This condo is so creaky and loud. And it's always cold. My living room is tiny, and I have no view. A beach house *would* be nice.

I shove another cookie into my mouth and stare at the wall. This is my life. Alone. Perpetually single. Nothing to look forward to, except eating cookies in my nightgown in the dark. How fun.

Still, I'm scared. I don't like change. I don't like not knowing what's going to happen next. I like to control things. The only problem is I've controlled myself right into being a hermit. If I didn't go to work at the restaurant, I'd probably be considered agoraphobic.

What would it be like to step into Monica's shoes for a while? Well, the shoes she wore when she was alive and well. Not her current shoes. Do people wear shoes in heaven? This is a question nobody has probably asked before.

I take one last sip of milk before pouring the rest down the drain and walking back upstairs. It's going to be a very long night.

NEW YEAR'S EVE. One of the worst days of the year for me.

I always try to stay off social media on this day. Everyone is planning their fun events and talking about the exciting new year ahead. Of course, most of those who make resolutions won't stick to them anyway, myself included, so I don't do it anymore.

Monica used to host the most elaborate New Year's Eve parties, complete with themes. One year it was eighties themed, another year it was your favorite movie. I never went to them. I'm not what one would call a socially adept person. I wish I was. I've often dreamed of walking into a party, waving and smiling at all of my admirers. Instead, I usually walk into a party and hide in the corner or the bathroom.

I don't know why I've always felt like this. To me, everybody else seems to have it so together. They seem so happy and well adjusted. I just feel awkward when I get around large groups of people.

Monica allowed me to be who I am. She was my best friend regardless of how different we were.

The way I already miss her is staggering. She was the closest person to me, and it's hard to imagine going through the rest of my life without her.

Sure, I have my daughter, and what a blessing she is! But she's just starting her adult life, and I can't be a burden on her. Eventually, I'll have to find at least one new friend, right? The problem is, that person won't be Monica.

I lay back on the sofa, my head resting on the cushy, bright yellow throw pillow Mon gave me for my last birthday. She said my house was too neutral, and I needed a pop of color in my life. I think it was more of a metaphor than decorating advice. I now realize *she* was the pop of color in my life.

All she wanted was for me to finish her list.

That thought has been rolling around in my head since we left the lawyer's office. How can I say no? How can I end our earthly friendship like that? I feel so guilty. Monica knew I would, of course. Making me feel guilty was her superpower. She could get me to do anything using guilt.

"You okay?" I hear Annie say as she comes downstairs. She looks all bright-eyed and bushy-tailed, while I look like death warmed over. Lack of sleep will do that to a middle-aged woman.

Middle-aged. *Beyond* middle-age, I guess, unless I'm planning to live to one-hundred.

"I'm fine. Just tired."

She sits in the armchair across from the sofa. The beige one with the little embroidered dragonflies on it. Monica hated that chair. Every time she came over, she unraveled some of them. Now there are only sporadic dragonflies on the chair. It made me mad at the time, but now it makes me smile.

"Do you have any plans tonight?"

I let out a loud laugh. "I plan to be disappointed in myself, as is customary."

"Oh, Mom," she groans at me. "Why don't you go out for once?"

I sit up and stare at her like she's speaking another language. "And where would I go? The club? That bar down the street?"

She shrugs her shoulders like it's no big deal. "Sure! Why not?"

"Because I'm not a lounge lizard," I say, falling back on the sofa again. I stare at the ceiling fan. I need to clean the blades. They look dusty. Maybe I can do that tonight.

"Okay, I don't even know what that means."

"That's because you're still young and vital," I say, sighing. "All of your skin is still tight. All of your hormones are still pumping through your veins. Meanwhile, my skin is starting to look like crepe paper, and my ovaries are two dried-up, shriveled raisins."

She stands up. "Okay, enough! You're just feeling sorry for yourself now."

I laugh. "Don't try to channel your Aunt Monica."

"I gave it a shot," she says, throwing her hands up. "I'm about to leave. I'll see you tomorrow."

I sit up again. "Wait. Where are you going?"

"Don't you remember? I told you I'm going on a trip with some of my girlfriends from high school.

We're meeting at a cabin in the mountains, and we're ringing in the new year at a vineyard party."

Wow, that sounds both nice and like too much work.

"Be very careful, Annie. There are bears in the mountains, you know."

She rolls her eyes. "Yes, Mom, I know about the bears."

I stand up and follow her to the door. "And there will be so many drunk drivers on the roads tonight. I really wish you'd stay closer to home…"

She turns to me and puts her hands on my shoulders. "Mom, I'm twenty-two years old. I know all of this. You have to calm down."

"I just worry."

"I know. We all know. Aunt Monica knew, and that's why she's asking you to do the bucket list. Her last wish is to break you out of this anxious spiral you're in all the time."

"By making me do things that cause anxiety?"

Annie smiles. "Yes. It makes perfect sense to me."

"Well, it makes no sense to me," I say, hugging her tightly. "Please be careful. And text me a bunch. Let me know you're alive. And don't stop at sketchy gas stations or rest stops. And no drinking and driving."

Annie salutes me. "Yes, ma'am!"

As I watch her walk to her car, my stomach clenches. This is going to be a long night.

By SEVEN O'CLOCK, my ceiling fan is dusted, and I'm bored out of my mind. I keep seeing all of my Facebook friends doing fun things for New Year's Eve, and I'm sitting on my sofa watching reruns of TV shows from the eighties.

There are brief moments of time that I think Monica and Annie are right. Maybe I am in a rut. Maybe I do need to be brave and try new things. Then I shove more potato chips into my mouth and squash the emotions.

As I scroll through my phone during a commercial break, I see a girl I knew from high school. She was a nerd back then, with frizzy red hair and thick glasses. Now, she looks like a supermodel, and her husband is gorgeous. He's a surgeon, and she's an entrepreneur.

Like the stalker I am, I comb through her photos and old posts. I see the progression of her being that shy, nerdy girl in school to now owning multiple investment properties. I see the trips she went on, some alone. I see her beautiful house, and her adorable kids.

A pain hits my stomach like a knife. It's probably the two bags of potato chips I've scarfed down, but it could also be the jealously and regret I feel. What have I done with my life?

Guilt washes over me as I think about how Monica won't get a chance to finish living her life. Yes, she did a lot of things, but she didn't get to finish. Unfinished business is the worst.

And then there's the guilt I feel over raising Annie while struggling with my insecurities and anxieties. Thankfully, she's an independent young woman, seemingly without a care in the world. I shouldn't be jealous of my own daughter, but I am.

Without giving myself time to change my mind, I stand up and grab my keys and purse. I'm going to that bar down the street. I'm going to have some wine and ring in the new year with other people, even if I don't know them. I'm going to be brave... or possibly slink back home in half an hour and look for that other bag of chips I hid above the refrigerator in that little cabinet nobody uses.

ONCE I ARRIVE at the bar, I remember I don't like bars. I don't even drink that often. Monica loved wine. She drank it all the time, and she knew all the different types. She would smell it and swish it around in her glass. Sometimes, I did it too, but I had no idea why I was doing it.

I stand outside the door of the little bar and debate going back home. Why is this so hard for me? I'm a grown woman of almost fifty years of age. Surely I can go inside a bar, sit on a stool, and have a glass of wine?

Forcing my feet to move forward, I open the door. The place is loud and packed with people who are happily getting toasted on their favorite alcohol. Yeah, it's not my favorite kind of place, but this is personal growth, right? If I can do this, then maybe I can do Monica's bucket list.

"Hey there," a gross sweaty man says as soon as I enter. He's leaning against a pillar near the front door, and it looks like he hasn't bathed in a few weeks. What a catch.

"Excuse me," I say as I push past him. This is like a house of horrors or one of those haunted houses where all kinds of scary things jump out as you walk through. Gross guy. Drunk guy. Smelly guy. Finally, I make my way to the bar and take the only seat left.

On my right side is a fairly normal looking fella wearing a suit. On my left is an obviously drunk girl who is focused on flirting with the bartender. I have to admit, he's pretty handsome. If I wasn't scared of my own shadow, I'd flirt with him, too. But I don't flirt because it's not a talent I possess. When I try to flirt, I act like a person who's just been let out of the mental ward and has never met another human being before.

"Do you like motorcycles?" drunk girl asks the bartender. He continues making drinks and basically ignoring her. She doesn't seem to care. She just smiles and fidgets around on the bar stool, coming within millimeters of falling off of it several times.

"What'll you have?" he asks me.

"Um…" Why the thought hadn't occurred to me that he would ask for my drink order… at a bar… is beyond me.

"You haven't been here before, have you?" he asks, smiling slightly. He's way younger than me and way out of my league. Why this godlike creature is pouring shots and dealing with drunks is baffling.

"No. I didn't have any New Year's plans, so…"

"Well, that's sad. No boyfriend? Husband?"

"Nope, afraid not."

"Yeah, my mom is newly single, so I know it's hard."

Did he just compare me to his *mother*? Surely, I'm not old enough to look like his mother?

"I'll just have a glass of Chardonnay," I say, eager to get him out of my sight. His mother? Seriously? He walks to the other end of the bar and I groan.

"That had to hurt." I turn to see the guy in the suit smiling as he drinks something brown.

"Excuse me?"

"Flirting with the bartender, and then he compared you to his mother," he says, laughing between sips.

"He didn't compare me to his mother. It was just a comment."

"I beg to differ."

"Here you go. Let me know if you need anything else," the bartender, whose name tag says Brendan, says as he slides the glass in front of me. Never have I wanted alcohol more in my life.

"Excuse me? Brendan, right?" The man in the suit is flagging down the bartender that I desperately want to leave.

"Yeah?" Brendan turns and leans against the counter.

"A moment ago, were you comparing this lovely lady to your mom?"

Brendan's eyes widen. "Oh, I'm sorry. I didn't mean to… I'm terrible with guessing ages. My mom is forty-eight. I'm sure you're not that old."

I want to crawl out of the bar, but I fear for my life if I do since there are all manner of disgusting things on the floor. Is that an old burrito over there?

"Please ignore what he said. I did not say that," I protest. "I don't know this guy, and I'm pretty sure he's three sheets to the wind."

"Three sheets to the what?" suit guy says.

"Drunk. You're drunk."

"I'm not drunk," he says as Brendan thankfully disappears again. "I don't get drunk."

"Sure. Whatever. Just stay over there."

"Why are you so uptight?"

"Is this how you always talk to women? Because if it is, I can see why you're alone."

His face grimaces for a moment, and I see I've hit a nerve. It's probably not good to argue with strange men in bars when you have to find your way home alone later.

"Look, I'm sorry. I had a bad day, and I shouldn't take it out on you."

I pause for a moment, waiting for the punchline. It doesn't come.

"Apology accepted." Who cares? I'm never going to see this doofus again, anyway. I mean, he is a cute doofus. He's actually like magazine cover handsome. But I won't tell him that because his head seems big enough already. "So, what went wrong in your day?"

"I'm not here for therapy." Ah, back to being a jerk.

"Fine. I'll tell you all my woes, and you can just sit quietly."

"Whatever." He takes another long drink.

"My best friend died a few weeks ago. She was my only friend, honestly. I've been widowed for fifteen years and haven't dated. I live alone, and I normally spend New Year's Eve sitting in my pajamas while I eat as much food as possible and dread the new year."

"Yikes."

"Right? Oh, and my friend has a beach house and a bunch of money she left me."

"And that's bad?"

"No, except she wants me to finish her crazy bucket list before she would've turned fifty in less than seven months."

"And you don't want to do that?"

47

I stare at him. He has crystal clear blue eyes that feel like they're going to hypnotize me. "No, I don't want to do that."

"Because you're scared?" He doesn't say it in an accusatory manner. He says it like he understands somehow.

"Yes." Why am I telling this perfect stranger all my inner thoughts? Two sips of wine, and I'm confessing all my sins.

"What do you want your obituary to say?"

"What?"

"Like, if you died tomorrow, what do you want people to say about you?"

"That's kind of morbid, don't you think?"

He shrugs his shoulders. "Maybe, but it's something to think about."

I think for a moment. "I want to be remembered as a good mother."

"Too safe."

"Okay, I want to be remembered as being generous and kind."

"All good things. But do you want people to also say... Wait, what's your name?"

"Jill."

He smiles slightly. "Jill." I don't know why he's saying my name like he's tasting the most delectable pastry he's ever had. He clears his throat. "Do you want people to say Jill lived life to the fullest?"

"Of course."

"I mean you don't want people to say Jill was anxious and wasted her life, do you?"

"Nobody would say that. What's your name?"

"Levi."

I giggle. "You don't look like a Levi."

"And what does a Levi look like?"

"Lots of denim."

"Funny."

"Works on a farm. Rides horses."

"How do you know I don't ride horses?"

"You just don't seem like the type with your fancy suit and nice shoes," I say, leaning back. I can't believe I'm talking to this guy like this. Normally, I find it very hard to make conversation with strangers. It's why I never have yard sales. Well, that and I don't have the energy.

He turns back toward his drink and chugs the rest of it, setting the glass back down on the bar with a thud. "I was at a funeral."

A huge lump forms in my throat, causing my voice to sound like a frog is stuck in it. "Oh, jeez. I'm sorry. And on New Year's Eve?"

"Yeah, well, many people don't actually choose

their death date," he says, giving me the worst case of side eye.

"Sorry." I might as well just pull my foot straight up and into my mouth. "As you can tell, I don't socialize a lot."

Surprisingly, that generates a smile out of Levi. He looks much better when he smiles. Maybe I should stop drinking wine now.

"Then maybe you should do it more?"

"Maybe. Although, this is the most uncomfortable thing I've made myself do in a long time."

"So, are you going to do your friend's bucket list?"

"I don't know."

"You should," he says, before putting cash on the counter and standing up.

"You think so?"

"Listen, you seem nice, but you're living too safely."

"And you live on the edge?" I ask, looking him up and down.

"Oh, darlin', if you only knew," he says, winking. Darlin'? Where did that come from? Why do I kind of like it? That settles it. No more wine.

"You're not seriously going to drive after drinking, are you?"

"Uber," he says, holding up his phone. "My ride is three minutes away."

"You're taking an Uber? Isn't that kind of dangerous?"

He shakes his head. "Oh, Jilly." My heartbeat speeds up as he walks away.

"Hey, wait! Why did you call me Jilly?"

He turns back and tilts his head to the side. "I don't know. It just seemed... right. Goodnight."

Before I can say anything else, he's out the front door and slipping into the backseat of a small blue car. I sit back down and stare at his empty seat, feeling an unexpected void. Was it just because he called me Jilly? Or was I actually connecting with that guy? I'll never know, I guess.

I can't think much longer about it before sweaty guy plops down on the empty stool. "Hey, pretty lady. Mind if you buy me a drink?" He laughs loudly at his own joke. That's my cue to pay for my wine and slip quickly out the front door.

CHAPTER 3

J sit up in bed like a bolt of lightning, my heart pounding. I hate that dream. I relive it over and over like I have for the last fifteen years.

Annie is seven years old, and she's playing in front of the TV with her dolls. She always loved dolls. We must've had two dozen dolls littering our house at any given time.

Jesse, my husband, is up on a ladder outside the living room window, trying to remove the Christmas lights I insisted we hang that year. I've regretted that decision ever since that day.

I'm standing in the kitchen washing dishes, but I have a clear line of sight through the living room and out that window. I can see the bottom of the ladder, and then I hear a loud thud. Annie screams as she stares out the window, and I run toward her in what seems like slow motion. I can't get there fast enough.

And then I see him, laying lifeless on our front lawn. He's fallen from the roof, which is two stories up. I scream so loud that I scare myself. I tell Annie to call for an ambulance, which is something we've drilled into her head since she could reach the phone.

I run outside, and he looks like he's asleep. He's not moving. I see no blood. I shake him and scream. I beg him not to leave. But I think he's already left me. There was no time to say goodbye. There was no time to say I'm sorry about the Christmas lights. There was no time.

The Jill I was that day died with him. I was never super adventurous, but I felt safe with Jesse. I felt accepted. Even though we were in marriage counseling when he died, I thought we'd make it. I thought we'd be okay.

This dream takes it out of me every time I have it, which is usually once a month like clockwork. Now, I've added dreams about Monica too, so most nights end up like this with my heart racing and sweat raining down my body.

I reach over and check my phone to make sure Annie is in a safe place. It looks like she's still at the cabin with her friends. I hope she's being careful. I wonder if she knows to lock up her trash so bears aren't attracted to her cabin?

I lay back down flat on my back and stare up at the ceiling. I can't see it, of course. It's still pitch black dark outside. I'm so tired of living my life alone. Sometimes it hits me like a baseball bat to the head. I feel the weight of nothingness. I feel the weight of loneliness. And now it's worse because at least I had Monica. She was my safe space.

I wonder why I can't have that soft place to fall at the end of a hard day. Why can't I have a man who looks at me with adoration? Why can't I have that sense of peace knowing when I wake up with a nightmare, there's someone there to comfort me?

Am I choosing to be lonely? It seems awfully sadistic, if that's the case. I often think I'm punishing myself, but I'm not sure for what. The human brain is an amazing, yet scary place to be.

I think about what Levi said at the bar. Maybe I am living too safely. Or maybe I just like to think about the way he said darlin' and Jilly. When Monica said it, I wanted to pinch her nose off. When he said it, I wanted to kiss his face. That seems out of the ordinary.

I get up out of bed and do the only thing I know to do. I'm going to text Monica. I have her phone, and I haven't disconnected service. I don't know why I haven't turned it off. I guess that means she's really gone.

Hey, Mon. How's heaven? Okay, that was a stupid thing to ask, but I do wonder.

I miss you. The world feels so heavy to carry alone.

I know you want to know if I'm going to do your bucket list. I can't believe you left that for me. I bet you had a good laugh thinking that up. If you were still here, I'd smack your arm for asking this of me. Maybe I'd kick you in the shin like I did that one time in sixth grade.

I'm scared, Mon. Of course, you knew I would be.

I talked to a cute guy at a bar last night. I still ended up ringing in the New Year in my living room with a tub of butter pecan, but I tried. I really did.

Okay, I'm stalling. You and I both know it.

I have to admit I want your beach house. I've always dreamed of living there. I'd rather have you back than anything else, but since God didn't give me that choice, at least I can remember you while sitting by the ocean. I feel like you want me to be there.

But how can I do this? I don't even know what you put

on that list, and I'm scared of it. I'm terrified I won't be able to do it, and I'm terrified that I will. I don't know how to be any other way than the way I am, Mon. I don't know how to be anyone else.

Well, I need to try to go back to sleep. I miss you. I'll never stop saying it. I wish I could wake up from this nightmare. I love you, my best friend forever.

As tears stream down my face, I press send, like it matters. It's not like the texts are going anywhere. I'm the only one reading them. Maybe that makes me mentally ill to write and read my own texts.

I jump back over to the GPS app, check on Annie, and then set my phone on the nightstand before laying back down. As I pull the covers up under my chin, I think about my options. Do the bucket list or don't? Live with the regret of not fulfilling Monica's last wish or live with the regret of dying in a horrible accident because I said yes. Well, I guess I wouldn't actually live with that regret since the regret itself involves being dead.

My brain hurts.

And now I have to pee because I'm almost fifty.

NEW YEAR'S DAY PASSES, and Annie returns home in time to say goodbye before heading back to college. It's always so hard to say goodbye, but I try not to show it because I want her to fly. I don't want her to be saddled worrying about her mother.

As I drive toward Dan's office, I still don't know what I'm going to say. I wish I had someone to talk to about this, but the person I used to talk to about these types of life choices is the one causing me to make the choice in the first place.

I park my car and get out, but I notice an older woman walking down the sidewalk. Well, she's more hobbling than walking, and she's got a caregiver with her. As she pushes her walker, I think about how terrible that would be to have a stranger taking care of you. Then I realize I'm setting up my life for that.

I can't expect Annie to care for me in my old age. She needs to live her life. Hopefully, she'll get married and have a bunch of grandkids I can spoil. Then it hits me. I won't be able to spoil them if I'm too afraid to do fun things with them. Who wants a stick-in-the-mud grandma who won't go to the fair or hike in the woods or go on a jet ski?

I take a deep, quivering breath and summon every ounce of courage in my body before walking straight into Dan's office building. I march past the receptionist who is calling my name, her voice full of alarm. I keep going.

"I'll do it!" I yell loudly as I open his door and proclaim my bravery. The only problem is, Dan is standing there wearing only his ill-fitting boxer shorts, and let me tell you - it's not a pretty sight.

Horrified in ways I can't describe without a thesaurus, I immediately cover my eyes and turn away like I've just seen the sun, and there are one-hundred naked, out of shape older men standing on it.

"What on earth?" he yells in shock, obviously startled and possibly on the verge of a heart attack.

"I'm sorry!" I say quickly. "I didn't expect you to be half-naked in here!"

"I'm not half-naked," he says, gruffly. "You can turn around now."

I turn back to see him fully dressed, wearing his normal Hawaiian shirt and khaki shorts.

"Why were you... like that... in your office?"

He sits down with a thud. "I had court this morning, so I had to wear a blasted suit. I hate those things. Now, what is it you came here for this morning?"

I try to shake off the sight of his spindly legs and

those too-tight boxer shorts. That vision is the thing nightmares are made of.

"I've decided to do it," I said, proudly smiling while my legs shake.

"Do what, dear?"

I stare at him in amazement. I guess I thought he was thinking about my predicament as much as I was.

"The bucket list."

He nods quickly. "Ah, yes, that's right. I had a bit of a fun time on New Year's Eve, so I'm still trying to get all my marbles back."

I wonder if the client he represented in court this morning knows that he doesn't currently have all his marbles.

"So, how do I get started?"

"Well, I suppose I can give you the first tasks, along with the login for Monica's blog. Now, let's see. I have it here somewhere." I don't know how this man made it through law school and passed the bar. I think that was probably the last time he passed a bar. "Here we go! This is the login information."

He hands me a thick, white index card with Monica's writing on it. I run my finger across it and force myself not to cry. She had the prettiest writing.

"And the list?"

"Not so fast. You don't get the list. Monica told me she wants you to have some surprises along the way."

"Of course she did."

"She said I could give you the first few. Then, you'll blog about them, show me your proof, and I'll give you more."

This feels like schoolwork. Very terrifying schoolwork.

"Okay, fine."

"You already know about a few. Salsa dancing, zip lining, crash a high school reunion, kiss a stranger…"

"Dear Lord, what am I agreeing to?" I mumble to myself for the millionth time since I decided to do it.

"Just a little FYI. There's a great ballroom dancing place over near Myrtle Beach. Maybe try them?"

"Myrtle Beach is at least ninety-minutes away."

"Oh… Did I not tell you? Monica said you can live at the beach house while you complete the list."

My stomach clenches. Live at Monica's house without her? It seems too soon to do that.

"Do I have to?"

"Well, no, you don't have to."

"It's too soon," I choke out, swallowing back tears. "Maybe later."

Dan nods. "I understand. Well, here you go. Those are the first four." I take them and continue standing there, knowing that the moment I leave his office, I'm committed. "Is there anything else, Jill? I sort of have a call…"

I can tell he's trying to get rid of me. "No, that's all. Thanks."

I walk out of the office and back out onto the sidewalk before looking down at the four envelopes in my hand. Although I know what's inside each of them, it doesn't make it any easier. I have to overcome my fears, and the one person who made that easier is the only one who can't help me.

I PARK my car in front of the ballroom dancing studio and pry my sweaty hands off the steering wheel. I can't believe I'm doing this. My anxiety is at an all-time high. How am I going to do the even harder things on Monica's bucket list if even going salsa dancing is hard?

As I enter the dance studio, I feel parts of my body shaking from anxiety. My heart is pounding so hard that I fear it'll just explode in my chest. Surely that would warrant a trip to the ER?

The room is dimly lit, like a nightclub in the heart of Cuba. Of course, how would I know? I've never been to Cuba. But, if there are dimly lit nightclubs in Cuba, I feel like this place could fit in.

The sound of Latin music fills the space, and it pulsates through my body. I decide to try to blend in with the other dancers, but then I realize I'm the only one wearing yoga pants and an oversized "I'm with stupid" t-shirt. I stick out like a sore thumb in the middle of a sea of women wearing tight dresses and high heels.

Then I notice the men. Dear Lord Almighty. Where did these men come from? Because I sure as heck have never seen any in the wild. It looks like the instructor just brought them in on a boat from Italy or other countries where incredibly hot men reside.

They are all tall, muscular, and wearing the tightest pants I've ever seen. Are they all in some sort of club? And, if so, how do I apply for membership?

As the class begins, the instructor - who thankfully hasn't noticed I'm new even though I look like I live under a bridge in a children's fantasy book -

pairs us up. Now, I'm excited. I'll get to touch one of these godlike creatures, and I won't even care if he sweats on me.

Suddenly, the door swings open, and the light from the lobby area obscures my view. When it closes, I see a man who can only be described as the exact opposite of the other guys there.

"Sorry I'm late," he says in an accent I can't identify.

"Stop being late, Larry," the instructor, who is a beautiful Latina woman with an accent sure to drive any man wild, says. "Now, go there. Pair with her."

Me? Oh no. Not me. He looks as though he hasn't showered in a week. Is that gel in his hair? Oil? Did he put it there, or did it just... accumulate?

But his hair and unshowered-ness aren't the only problems.

"You new here?" he asks me, without putting much space between our faces. I definitely enjoy way more space between my face and his. His breath wafts towards me, and I'm suddenly transported to an Italian restaurant without the good food. More like the bathroom of an Italian restaurant that hasn't been cleaned in three years. Has he been munching on onions and garlic during his ride over here?

The music starts, and he grabs my waist. He

wiggles and gyrates, and this certainly doesn't feel like any salsa I've ever seen on TV. I silently swear at Monica for making me do this.

The music picks up, and I try to keep up with Larry's fast-paced, frenetic movements. I feel like I'm having some kind of attack. This surely isn't dancing. My feet get tangled up in his more times than I can count, and my anxiety ramps up. We suddenly stumble into another couple who is actually doing the salsa, and they fall to the ground. I'm completely mortified as the entire class stops to stare at us. I feel like a sideshow.

But then Larry decides the dancing shall continue before the other couple even makes it to an upright position. He pulls me close once again and continues stepping on my toes every few seconds. I wince in pain, asking him to be more careful, but his limited knowledge of English - or his inability to care that he's doing permanent damage to my toes - causes the toe stomping to continue.

When I was a kid, my mom told me I needed to stand up for myself. There was a girl at school who was bullying me because I had a giant gap in my teeth, and my own mother told me to clock her if she said it again. My mother was a bit rough around the edges.

But then - and now, apparently - I tend to let people walk all over me. And Larry is literally walking all over me. My toes are now smashed like pancakes, but good old Larry is obliviously cutting a rug as he shakes his hips and makes grunting noises one would normally hear near the pigpen on a farm.

When the class finally comes to an end, Larry winks at me, pulls a comb from his pocket and runs it through his shiny hair. He thankfully disappears without a word, like a smelly, oily mirage.

I quickly hurry to my car, eagerly anticipating a hot bath and possible foot surgery. This bucket list thing might actually kill me.

"OH, MOM, I'M SO SORRY," Annie says as she looks back at me on our daily FaceTime video call. I can see she's struggling not to laugh because her face is turning red.

"You can laugh. It's okay."

She bursts out in hysterics and falls back against her bed where she's sitting. I listen to her belly laughs for a few moments before she sits upright and wipes tears from her eyes.

"I think I'm okay now. I was just imagining that

man stepping on your toes. Why didn't you pull away and tell him you were done?"

I shrug my shoulders. "I don't know. Your Aunt Monica always said I'd let people pull the hairs out of my nose and stand there smiling about it. I guess she was right."

It's one of those qualities I hate about myself. I want to be one of those powerful women who stand up for themselves and don't take any guff. Instead, I'm a passive pushover who will allow permanent toe disfigurement instead of just saying "stop".

"So, what's next up on the agenda?"

"Ziplining. I've got a reservation for Friday."

Annie's mouth drops open. "That's a big one for you. Where are you going?"

"There's a place about an hour from here that will let me zip through the forest canopy," I say before hanging my head.

"Are you scared?"

"Petrified is more like it. Come with me?"

"Mom, you know I would if I could, but I have a test that day."

"Maybe I can switch it to Saturday."

"I'll be out of town for the weekend with some of my sorority sisters. I'm sorry."

Who wants to hang out with their boring old

mother, anyway? I feel so lonely without Monica here to hold my hand through life.

"It's okay. I have to learn to do things on my own. Don't worry about me." I force a smile and then ask about her classes. I don't want my daughter to be saddled with me. I have to figure out how to change my ways, at least a little, if I ever want any hope for a real life.

CHAPTER 4

I stand at the base of the tree and wonder if I've lost my mind. As I stare up at the rustling canopy above, my heart pounds in my chest like a jackhammer. My palms are sticky with sweat again, and I don't know if I can do this.

Monica made this list for me, and that is a fact I remind myself of repeatedly. I have to honor her memory. I can't let her down. I did the salsa dancing, but dancing with a smelly guy is a far cry from letting strangers strap me into a death harness and fling me over the trees through the forest. This is a whole different ballgame.

The thought of even climbing up there is making my stomach churn, and I fear that burrito I ate last night might make an encore appearance.

I can't shake the feeling that something awful is going to happen. And wouldn't I be a big dummy for not listening to my own intuition?

I'm looking for any way out of this insanity when one of the instructors walks over to me. He seems nice enough with his sandy brown hair and big white teeth, but he looks like he could be my son. Surely, he doesn't have enough experience to be throwing people off perfectly good platforms to their death.

Moments later, I find myself signing the waiver form that says they can kill you and not get into legal trouble. Again, I don't stand up for myself. I should've said, "Why, no, dear young boy, you may not take my life for your entertainment purposes." Instead, I just sign on the bottom line like the big sucker I am.

Before I know it, I'm standing on the platform of death mentally going over all the greatest moments of my life. Getting married. Having Annie. And then there was... Wait, was that it? I mean, those were great things and all, but didn't I do more?

I continue struggling to think of any real accomplishments other than learning how to work my new phone last year, and I come up with a big, fat goose egg of nothingness. Before I can think too hard about my lack of exciting life events, the young man - whose name is Connor - starts strapping me in.

"How many times have you done this?" I ask.

He smiles his big toothy grin. "You're my first."

My mouth drops open. "What?"

"It was just a joke, ma'am."

"Not a funny one," I mutter back, suddenly realizing this kid literally has my life in his hands.

"Sorry. Don't be scared. There's nothing to it."

"Have you done it?"

"Tons of times. I love the thrill and rush of adrenaline!"

"Well, I don't."

He tightens up the straps and double checks his work. "Why are you here then?"

"I promised a friend."

He looks around. "Where is your friend?"

I point upward. "Up there. At least I think so."

He stares up at the sky, and a plane happens to fly over at the same time. "In that airplane?"

I worry for the future of our society. "Yep."

A few more guys come check my harness, which makes me feel somewhat better because Connor has no common sense, apparently. Moments later, they say, "It's go time!"

Suddenly, I'm flying through the air, the wind

blowing my hair and the smell of pine filling my nostrils. I close my eyes at first out of sheer terror. I hear someone screaming. Oh wait, that's me.

The rush of air whooshes past me as I am propelled forward, my heart racing faster than is medically advisable. My newly formed wrinkles are pushed back like I'm getting a free facelift, and my stomach feels as though it's heading upward into my chest.

Something tells me to open my eyes, and when I do, I can't believe what I see. The trees soar beneath me, and birds swoop and dive around me. I feel like I'm flying, and the way it invigorates me comes as a total surprise.

In that moment, all my fears disappear. It's a feeling I've never had before, and maybe never will again, so I decide to savor it. I'm not scared right now. I'm as free as I've ever felt in my life. It's like the fear was so large that it exploded, and all that was left was peace. I don't think I've ever felt such peace as I zoom past each tree in the forest.

I'm lost in the wonder of it all, and I feel jealous of birds now. What must life be like to feel so free all the time?

I feel alive.

As I reach the end of the zip line, thudding onto

the wooden platform, I'm a little sad. Mostly, I'm proud. I did it. I drove there alone. I climbed up there alone. And I just flew like a bird alone. I just faced a fear and conquered it. I feel more confident than I have in years, or maybe ever.

Is it possible that one simple thing like a zip line could make me more courageous? I guess time will tell. For now, I'm basking in the afterglow of my accomplishment.

As I walk back to my car, I hear the rustling of the leaves beneath my feet and feel the soft flow of wind in my hair, and I think of Monica. She would've slayed this for sure. I have to believe she's in heaven right now cheering me on and bragging to all her angel friends about how her anxious friend just did a zip line by herself. The thought makes me smile.

I STAND in Dan's office once again, waiting for my marching orders.

"Have you done the other two things?"

"I'm working up to it, Dan. Crashing the class reunion and kissing a stranger are both very outside of my comfort zone at the moment."

"I don't know if this follows Monica's rules…"

"I don't really think Monica has much to say about it right now. Besides, she didn't stipulate anything about a particular order in her original letter."

Dan thinks for a moment and finally relents. "Fine. Take these two. But I have no idea what they say."

"Fair enough." I turn to walk back toward the hallway. "You know, I did the zip lining."

He smiles slightly. "How was it?"

"Terrifying."

"Sorry to hear that."

"But exhilarating," I say quickly. "I think Monica would've been proud of me."

He nods. "I believe when people pass away, they can still see us from the other side. Maybe it's just wishful thinking, but it's what I believe. And that means Monica can see you, and she's very proud, Jill. I just know it."

"Thank you. I needed to hear that," I say before quickly hurrying to my car and dissolving into a puddle of tears.

WHEN I WOKE up this morning, my heart was already racing, and it felt like my stomach was tied up in a bunch of knots. I've already done the salsa dancing and the zip lining, so it seems like I should get less anxious but today, with the thought of going up in a hot-air balloon by myself, I'm not feeling so great.

I'm worried that the balloon is just going to pop in the sky, and I'm going to come plummeting down to earth creating a large splat on the ground. I need to lose at least twenty-five pounds so the splat would be significantly larger than people are expecting. That'd be super embarrassing.

I asked Annie if she could come with me today, but she's far too busy at school. I need to do things myself, anyway. After all, this is my best friend's bucket list, and I'm supposed to be doing these in honor of her. But I'm still scared.

I don't know if this anxiety is ever going to go away. I don't know if the fear that I live with on a daily basis about literally everything is ever going to truly get better. Is this whole thing that Monica has required me to do really going to help me be a better person? To live a better life? I don't know, but I do know that I need to get in the car and head towards the place where we're going to launch the hot-air balloon.

I can't believe I'm doing this. What if that fire that goes up inside the balloon actually catches my hair on fire? That seems like it would be bad. I don't think I would enjoy that.

I'm driving now toward the hot-air balloon location, and then I start wondering about other things like what if it flies too close to a tree, and we get stuck? When I was a kid, I was constantly letting go of balloons I got at the carnival, and they always got stuck in trees and died a slow, painful death. Then when winter would come, I would just see the string hanging there like a lifeless reminder of the once beautiful balloon I wanted so badly.

I'm still kind of worried about the balloon catching on fire. I'm also worried that the basket will tip, and I will plummet to my death.

These all seem like completely logical worries. I can't believe other people are not worried about this, but when I get there, I see a long line of cars and people waiting to go up in one of these death traps. Now I'm one of those people as I'm greeted by a cheerful team of balloon operators. I'm not really sure what you call someone who works on a hot-air balloon. A pilot? A disappointment to their family?

Other people seem completely unfazed by the idea that they're going to fly hundreds of feet off the ground. Wait, is it thousands of feet? How do we keep from ending up stuck to the wing of an airplane?

All I know is that it's a giant flammable bag, and I'm willingly getting into it just to possibly get a beach house and my best friend's bank accounts. This seems like a really stupid idea, but apparently I'm going to do it, anyway.

They hand me a waiver to sign. Why do these places always do that? The zip line guys did the same thing. It's like the craziest thing to think that human beings willingly sign a piece of paper saying, "Hey if you kill me, no biggie."

I mean, the paper literally says "death or serious injury may occur". Why am I signing up for this? Why does anybody sign up for something like this? I'm questioning all of humanity at this point because it just seems entirely crazy that we say, "hey, let me go do this stupidly dangerous thing to get an adrenaline rush". I don't get it, but apparently I'm going to do it. I've come this far. I will not back out. Now I've signed my name to the death paper. I've strapped on my death harness, and now I'm climbing into the basket of death. The *flammable* basket of death.

As the balloon inflates with hot air, I feel my stomach churning with more anxiety than ever. I hold on tightly to the edges of the basket. As I watch the ground slowly slip away and get further from view, my heart is still pounding so hard and so fast that I'm afraid I might need to call for medical intervention.

"Hey lady, are you okay?" the young man piloting the balloon of death asks me.

"Not really." I close my eyes, hoping my brain has forgotten that I'm floating straight into space.

He says nothing else because what's he going to do? Lower me to the ground with some kind of pulley system?

I wonder why heart racing is my biggest anxiety symptom. Well, that along with sweaty hands and the absolute fear that I'm about to die. But then, as we float even higher and I finally open my eyes, something amazing happens. My fear starts to dissipate again just like it did when I was zip lining. Instead, it's replaced by this sense of wonder and awe as I look at all the beautiful scenery around me. I let out the breath I've been holding since I got here.

Sure, I'm high in the air and that's kind of freaking me out, but I'm able to overcome that worry while I look at all the beautiful things like the trees, the ground, the flowers, the birds that are now flying at eye level. The world just looks so different from up here. It's much more beautiful and peaceful.

It's certainly better than what I see on the nightly news or the internet. The trees look like tiny little specks, and the roads are like thin little ribbons running through the forest. People look like ants going about their business. I look out at the horizon, taking in the beautiful rolling hills and the green forests. The sun is just beginning to peek over the treetops and it casts this warm glow over everything, and the sky is a mixture of beautiful pinks and oranges this morning.

I just couldn't be more thankful that I've been given this opportunity to do this, and a part of me can't believe I'm even thinking that thought. Has someone overtaken my brain? Has Monica somehow come back from heaven and possessed me? Am I suddenly getting brave?

I decide not to think about it too hard and just enjoy the moment. I feel close to my best friend right now, and I just want to treasure this moment.

As I sit in front of my laptop at my kitchen table, I struggle to come up with the right words. I'm not really a writer. I did okay in high school, but I certainly never planned to be the proud new owner of an adventure blog. Boy, are these readers going to be sorely disappointed with my views about adventure.

I have to play catch up and write several posts about Monica's death, salsa dancing, zip lining, and now the hot-air balloon. It feels surreal to list them out like that. I can't believe I've done any of those things.

I first write the news of my best friend's death. It's so hard to talk about, much less express in writing. The post is short and probably a bit too much to the point, but I want to get it over with.

Once I publish it, I sigh with relief.

Thankfully, for each of the bucket list items, I've written about it on my phone just after finishing. Thank goodness for dictation. While each of the tasks were still fresh in my mind, I've talked about them. Now, I just need to transcribe my notes and clean them up.

I spend all morning doing this, downing way too many coffees in the process. I know better. I should drink decaf because the caffeine in these cups will send my heart rate spiraling ever upward.

My phone rings, and I'm happy to see it's Annie.

She went out to a party last night, and I stayed up way too late watching the GPS app to make sure she got home safely. Surprisingly, I fell asleep before she made it home and didn't get to check it again until three AM when I got up to pee. At almost fifty, I can't sleep through the entire night without getting up at least once. Ah, the challenges of getting older.

"Hey there! I'm surprised you're up this early after your party last night."

Annie chuckles. "It wasn't a rager, Mom."

I have no idea what that means. "What's going on?"

"Well, one of my professors has the flu."

"Oh no. Were you exposed?"

"No. But, I have an idea."

"Okay, what?"

"Well, you know how you have that one bucket list item you've been avoiding?"

"There's more than one, honey."

"The one about crashing a high school reunion?"

Oh yes. That one seems almost as terrifying as kissing a stranger. What was Monica thinking?

"Well, I was looking on Facebook, and I saw Stacy's mom got invited to her thirty-fifth high school reunion. It's in Myrtle Beach."

"So?"

"It's perfect! You won't know anyone there, and we can go to the beach!"

"Wait. You want to go with me?"

"I don't have class until late next week, and the reunion is this Friday night. Come on! Let's live on the edge and knock this one out together."

I want to say no way. I want to keep procrastinating. But my daughter is actually interested in hanging out with me. She wants to go on a trip with me. I can't say no to that.

"Okay, let's do it!" I say with tons of fake enthusiasm.

"Really? That's awesome!" She's genuinely excited to hang out with her boring old mom. Well, her mom did just zip line and fly through the air in a balloon. Maybe she's not quite as boring anymore.

"I'll find us a place to stay," she offers. I'm glad because it's been years since I traveled, and I don't know how to work those apps people use. I feel so old sometimes.

"Sounds good. I'll see you soon!"

As I hang up and look back at my computer, I try to mentally prepare myself for crashing a reunion. What will I say? How will I get myself and my daughter into a place where nobody knows us? This ought to be very interesting.

CHAPTER 5

J can't believe I'm standing here. I don't even like bars, yet I'm back at the one down the street. I don't even know why I came.

Yes, I do. For some reason, I'm looking for that guy I talked to last time. The one in the suit. The one who rubbed me the wrong way at first, but then made me want to chase him down the street when he left.

Maybe I should get my hormones checked. The last time I saw my doctor, he said I was in perimenopause so I'm boycotting him. What an awful thing to say to someone.

Thankfully, he gave me some hormone cream that helped a lot. Instead of wanting to sleep all day, I could finally function. Plus, I stopped crying all the time. For a while there, I thought I might become dehydrated from crying over sappy commercials and videos of soldier homecomings on Facebook.

I sit at the bar with my glass of wine and a basket of fries. Nothing says I don't know what I'm doing like a glass of wine and a basket of fries.

Every time the door opens, I crane my head to see if it's Levi. I don't know why I want to see him again. It's a Wednesday night in my small town, so it's not like there's a significant chance of seeing him again. Most people don't spend their weekdays sitting in a bar unless they should also be sitting at a support group meeting.

After an hour, I realize what I'm doing is silly and I should go home. But I stay. I'm tired of being alone all the time. It's crazy how it was comfortable to me for fifteen years, and now I suddenly can't stand it.

I used to abhor being around people, and now I'm starting to crave the connection. It's like I'm waking up out of a fog.

For so long after Jesse died, I wanted to crawl into myself and keep the world out. With the exception of Monica and Annie, I did just that. I didn't make friends, not even at work.

I did my job well at the restaurant, but I didn't make connections with people. It's not like people didn't try to be my friend, and a few guys asked me out on dates over the years, but I was so closed off that no one could break through my barrier.

I look down at my phone to see what time it is, and I see my home screen. It's me and Monica, sitting together on the beach last summer, drinking big frozen fruity drinks with umbrellas in them. I miss her so much it hurts.

Determined to get myself out of this poor-me slump, I wave for the bartender.

"What can I get you?" This is a different guy from last time. Not as cute, which is a good thing.

"See this drink?" I point to the picture.

"Yes."

"That's my friend who just died. I want something that looks like this so I can toast to her honor."

He smiles slightly. "I'm sorry about your friend. Let me see what I can put together."

"Thanks."

He walks to the other end of the bar and starts rummaging around.

"Sorry about your friend," a woman says from two stools down. She looks about my age and doesn't appear to be intoxicated. I guess those are the two criteria for being my friend these days - old and not drunk.

"Thank you."

She stands up and moves next to me. "Hope you don't mind if I sit here. There's a smelly guy down there, and he's giving me a migraine."

I lean over and look. "Oh, I know him. He sat beside me last time. I had to wash my clothes twice just to get the smell out."

She laughed. "Right? It's like he rolled in cow manure, and even that might be offensive to a cow."

"I'm Jill," I say, reaching out to shake her hand. I feel awkward. Is a handshake still a thing?

"I'm Lila. I know this sounds weird, but do you come here often?"

My stomach clenches. "Oh… I'm not… uh… I mean, you're very nice, but…"

Lila chokes on her sip of wine. "Oh no! That wasn't a pickup line. I was just asking because I've never been here before. I was just curious if you come here a lot."

I feel like a dork. "Sorry. I misunderstood."

"I can totally see why. I'm not used to a lot of social situations. I just got divorced after almost twenty years. I spent most of that time raising my two kids, so this is my first outing as a divorced woman."

"I'm not much help. I've been a widow for fifteen

RACHEL HANNA

years. This is only my second time here, and honestly I don't know why I'm here. I guess I'm tired of being alone."

"And then you lost your best friend? Mind if I ask how?"

"Cancer."

She shakes her head. "That stinks."

"Monica was a light. Everybody loved her. She was just one of those people that lit up every room. She was funny and adventurous, both things I am not."

"Don't sell yourself short. I bet you're funny."

I look at her, shaking my head. "I'm really not."

"I've been terrified sitting at this bar all night. I was just glad to see another woman who didn't look like a streetwalker or an ax murderer."

I laugh. "Same here."

"What do you think?" The bartender reappears in front of me holding a giant frozen drink, complete with an umbrella.

"Thank you! This is fantastic."

"Hey, I'll have one of those, too. I'm tired of wine," Lila says, pushing her glass away. "Thank goodness for Uber, huh?"

"I'm normally not much of a drinker, but I wanted to toast my friend. This drink looks just like the one in the picture." I hold up my phone and show her the photo.

"It really does. Mind if I toast with you? I mean, I didn't know her, but you need another person's glass to clink, right?"

"Absolutely!"

We chat for a bit while the bartender makes another frozen drink for Lila. She seems very nice. It's the first time I've had a new friend since my school days, and even then they were few and far between. If Monica didn't bring me into her friend group, I would've lived as a hermit.

"So what do you do for a living?" he asks.

"Well, that's a bit up in the air for right now."

"What do you mean?"

"One reason I'm sitting here at a bar drinking away my feelings is because of what my best friend wrote in her will."

"Oh, that sounds intriguing. Tell me more."

"Monica was a very adventurous soul. She would do anything. Literally. She was one of those people who would bungee jump without even thinking about it. She jumped out of airplanes more times than I can count. So, when I went to the reading of her will, I wasn't expecting that she was going to ask me, the least adventurous person on the planet, to finish her bucket list."

Lila's mouth drops open."Seriously?"

"Seriously. She left me a bunch of sealed envelopes with tasks that I have to complete and blog about. If I get everything done before her fiftieth birthday, I inherit all of her money and her beach house on Pawley's Island."

"I wouldn't know whether to be happy, sad, or mad."

"Now you know how I feel. Sometimes, I miss her so much that it hurts. Actually, that's most of the time. Other times, I am angry at her for leaving me to do this. She knows how anxious I am. I don't know why she couldn't just leave me whatever she wanted to leave me without making me go through all of this."

"Maybe she was just trying to help you get rid of the anxiety. I'm sure she was worried that you'd spend the rest of your life in fear."

I nod my head. "I know that's the truth, logically at least. But it doesn't make it any easier when I'm doing these things alone and terrified. I've already zip lined, took a salsa dancing class, and I went up in a hot-air balloon by myself."

"I'll do some things with you!"

I stare at her, this complete stranger offering to do bucket list items with me. "What?"

"I mean, I don't want to intrude or anything. But if you need me to do some of the stuff with you, I'm more than willing. I'm not exactly the most adventurous person on the planet, but it sounds like you might be a little more scared than the typical person."

I laugh. "I have to admit, I'm scared of everything. I was widowed fifteen years ago, and I haven't even gone on a date since then."

Again, Lila's mouth drops open. "Wow. You must be really lonely sometimes."

I shrug my shoulders. "I have a wonderful daughter. She's twenty-two years old."

"Does she live with you?"

"No. She's at college about to finish up her degree, and then she'll be going out to live her life. She doesn't think I know, but I heard through the grapevine that she's had some job opportunities in California and Colorado. I know she won't be living close to me for the rest of her life, and that thought scares me to death. The thought of being alone forever. It's just a lot." I suddenly realize that I'm telling this complete stranger all of my innermost thoughts and feelings. She's probably going to run screaming out the door any minute now.

"I kind of understand. My kids are now adults about to start college. One of them will go to Seattle, the other one will be in South Florida. And now I'm going to be starting all over again without a husband. It's a little scary."

"At the end of the week, I'm doing one of the craziest things I've done in my life. Monica is making me crash a high school reunion."

Lila laughs. "Seriously? That sounds like it would be really fun. Are you doing that alone?"

"No. Actually my daughter has offered to come with me. I think she wants to see her mother make a fool of herself." I take a nice, long sip of my frozen drink, closing my eyes for a moment to remember what it was like to sit on the beach and drink daiquiris with Monica. People walking by would stare at us because we were laughing so hard.

"That's great that she wants to go with you. You shouldn't do everything alone. Listen, if you want someone to go with you to any of this, I'm more than willing. I need something to take my mind off of this nasty divorce. Hand me your phone. I'll put my number in there, and you can text me anytime."

I suddenly feel thankful I've met this person,

although I know next to nothing about her. It's just nice to have someone to talk to who kind of understands what I'm going through. I'm thankful for conversation, and a part of that is very sad.

"Here you go," the bartender says, sliding an identical drink in front of Lila.

"Thanks."

"So, I guess we should toast." Lila raises her glass in the air, as we clink them together.

"To Monica. May she be looking down at me now feeling proud *and* amused."

I CANNOT BELIEVE I am standing in the parking lot of a high school I've never been to, about to drag my daughter inside to pull off the lie of the century.

"Maybe I can talk to Dan and see if there's any way around doing this."

Annie laughs and punches me in the arm lightly. "Mom, quit trying to get out of this. It's going to be fun. You can pick out an alter ego."

"They're going to ask me to check in. And I don't know any of the names."

"We're just going to fly by the seat of our pants. Can't you imagine doing that for once in your life?"

I glare at her. "I already flew by the seat of my pants through the forest. Alone."

"Okay, not the same thing, but whatever."

I really hate how the younger generation says *whatever* all the time. Like that's the end of an argument? You can just say *whatever*, and somehow you won?

"That's just silly. I don't understand why this would have been on Monica's bucket list. It doesn't make any sense. This is the same woman who hiked the entire Appalachian Trail with a group of strangers."

"Maybe she just had some lingering little things she wanted to do, and they were boring, so she put them at the bottom of her list."

"I can't believe I'm going to do this."

"Have you opened the other envelope Dan gave you?"

"Not yet. Of course, I still have the one where I'm supposed to kiss a stranger. That sounds like something Monica would do, but I'm surprised she never did it."

"I'm sure Aunt Monica kissed strangers before. I don't know why she didn't check it off her bucket list."

I stare at the school one more time, watching the

sun start to set behind it. It's in Myrtle Beach, and the ocean is just a couple of blocks away. The sun sets on the other side of the road behind the school.

"I guess let's go inside. But if we get caught, I hope they aren't going to call the police or something."

"Mom, do you really think they're going to call the police because we try to go to a high school reunion?"

"I guess not. But stranger things have happened."

We walk toward the school, and a man smiles and greets us as he opens the door. We go inside to find a very busy lobby area with one long table. Instead of having to check in, there are tons of pre-filled name tags. I look around to see if I can find any blank ones where I can just make up a name, but no such luck.

"So we just need to get a name tag," Annie whispers.

"And what happens if the people show up and have no name tags? Or, worse yet, they run into us in the cafeteria and we're wearing their name tags?"

"Maybe they won't show up."

"So you're saying that we will just happen to pick the two people who don't show up?"

"I don't know! Why do you have to make everything so complicated?" Annie asks, throwing her hands in the air. I'm sure at twenty-two years old, all of this seems ridiculous. She wanted to come and have a fun time with her mother, and here I am making things stressful again.

"Okay, fine. We're just going to grab a couple of name tags and slip through the door. In fact, I'll just take a name tag, and I'll tell them you're my daughter. That way we don't have to steal two name tags."

"Whatever."

I want to smack her, but I refrain. We walk over to the table, and I scan the names. Which of these names sounds like it could be me? Katerina? No. Lois? No. I walk up and down the table trying to choose a name like it's going to be my name for the rest of my life.

After a few moments, I decide I will be Emma Eastwick for the evening. It sounds like some character from a movie. Let's just hope I look enough like Emma to pass the test. I have no idea what this woman looks like.

I stick on the name tag, and Annie and I hurry through the doors. For a moment, I think about taking it off so that nobody asks me questions, but I'm afraid that will get us kicked out. Monica didn't say how long we had to stay at this thing, but I have to stay long enough to write a blog post about it.

"Well, at least it looks like they've got some good food. Want to make a plate?"

"Yes. I'm starving."

We walk over to the long table with a huge buffet. I watch Annie as she piles her plate high with chicken fingers and chips, which just makes me feel like I'm going to gain five pounds from looking at it.

I opt for some finger sandwiches, potato salad, and plain shrimp. Even what I eat is boring.

We walk over to the corner and stand at one of the tall bar tables they brought in. The place is very loud with music playing, and everybody is in little groups talking to each other. I try to imagine what these people were like in high school. I'm sure they are standing in the same groups they were thirty-five years ago.

I try to just stay out of the way because the last thing I want is for somebody to come over and start talking to me like I'm Emma Eastwick. What if they ask me some crazy questions, and I don't know the answers?

"How was your food?"

"Amazing. Why didn't you get some of these

chicken fingers? I think they're beer battered. I don't know who catered this, but they did a great job."

I'm trying to listen to what Annie is saying, but all I can think about is getting out of here. I just know somebody's going to come over here any minute now and ask who I am and what I'm doing here. How embarrassing would it be to be thrown out of a high school reunion?

"I wonder how long we need to stay?"

"Mom, what are you going to write about if you don't take part in the reunion?"

"Take part how? I don't know what I'm supposed to be doing."

"You need to mingle around. Pretend to be Emma. Do some dancing. The blog post needs to be interesting so people believe you actually came here."

That reminds me to take some photos that I can use along with the blog post. I snap a few as I'm standing at the table, trying not to let anyone see me.

"Care for a glass of wine?" a woman asks, walking over to the table. She appears to work for the catering company, so I'm thankful that it's not somebody who's going to strike up a conversation with me.

"I would love one. Thank you."

Annie raises her hand. "One for me too, please."

The woman doesn't even ask for Annie's I.D., which I find very surprising. But we are at a reunion for people who've been out of high school for over three decades, so she probably doesn't assume anybody here is going to be under age.

We stand in the corner, eating our food and drinking wine for a good half hour. After a couple of glasses, I'm feeling pretty loose. Thankfully, Annie only has one glass so I don't have to worry about who's driving.

The looser I am, the easier this whole thing is going to be. Although, I can't rely on alcohol every time I have to do something hard. That's how people end up with a problem. I doubt Monica wanted me to become an alcoholic just because I was completing her bucket list.

"There's not many good-looking men around here," I suddenly say. Annie eyes me carefully.

"I think you've had enough wine."

"I'm fine! But look at all these guys. I have to wonder which ones were the popular ones back in high school. Was it that guy over there who's got the giant beer belly? Or maybe that one over there who's rocking the Dr. Phil hairdo?"

"Mom, hold your voice down," Annie says,

touching my arm. I've never been able to hold my alcohol. Wine gets me the tipsiest the fastest.

"You know, if I was smart, I would just go ahead and kiss the stranger here and kill two birds with one stone."

I can see a smile spreading across my daughter's face. She's totally up for this idea. I don't even know why I brought it up because I certainly don't want to kiss a stranger ever, and definitely not right now. As previously stated, this is a room full of dogs.

"I think you should do it. That way you don't have to keep worrying about it or talking about it every time I call you on the phone."

"Oh, I'm so sorry. I hate to interrupt your wonderful life with all of my problems," I say, sarcastically, a slight slur in my voice that I can't seem to get under control.

"Seriously. Find the least offensive looking guy in here, and go kiss him."

"And how do I know if he's married?"

"Well, now, that might be a problem."

"I know! You can be my private investigator," I say, slurring my words once again. I really need to drink a glass of water.

"What do you mean?"

"Go scope out the best-looking guy in here and

check his finger for a wedding band. See if a woman is hanging around him. Try to find somebody that is safe for me to kiss then run straight out that front door over there."

"Okay, if you say so," Annie says, laughing as she walks away. I see her go to all four corners of the room and then out into the lobby and back. She comes back, shaking her head.

"What's wrong?"

"Every guy here is either married or so ugly that I cannot allow you to kiss him."

"Darn! I was really hoping to get that over with."

We finish eating our food, and Annie says that I need to go dance a little bit to work off some of this wine. She's more than likely right, although I don't much feel like dancing. I feel like going home and crawling into my bed until morning.

But, I want to spend time with my daughter, so I agree to go out on the dance floor. They're playing eighties music, and I love eighties music. I feel myself dancing around, pumping my fists in the air, and I simply don't care. I don't know these people, and I'm a little more tipsy than I thought. It's amazing how a little alcohol can give you a lot of courage.

CHAPTER 6

*W*e dance in the middle of this large group of people, and Annie suddenly smiles. "I see a guy who just came in, and he's not bad looking. I'm going to go over there and see if I see a wedding ring or a woman." Before I can say anything, she slips away.

"Emma Eastwick?" This isn't good. Somebody has recognized me by my name tag, so I attempt to just ignore them. But this woman isn't giving up. She's tapping on my shoulder so much that I'm afraid she's going to break her finger.

I slowly turn around, smiling so big that my cheeks hurt. Let's hope that Emma Eastwick didn't have a large birthmark on her cheek, because then my cover is blown.

"Yes?" I say, playing as innocent as I can. The woman grins, so it's obvious that she doesn't recognize that I'm definitely not Emma.

"I can't believe you came! That's quite a long way that you traveled."

I nod my head slowly, pretending that I know where I live. But I don't know where I live because I'm not Emma. "Yes, it was a long way. But so worth it to see everybody."

"Do you still play?"

Play what? The guitar? The witch in the Broadway production of Wicked? Play with dolls?

"Not so much anymore," I say, unable to come up with anything else.

"Me neither. It's so hard to keep up with playing the flute when you have a family and other obligations."

The flute? Okay, so Emma Eastwick was a big nerd. That feels more like me.

"Right, absolutely." I'm trying everything to get her bored enough that she'll just walk away but it doesn't seem to be working. I notice nobody else is coming up to talk to her, so I'm thinking she must've been in the same group of friends I was in high school. The nerds. The outcasts.

Monica was the only reason I didn't get bullied.

She was in a popular crowd, and there was no way she was going to let anybody mess with her best friend. So although I didn't get invited to all the parties, and people didn't say hello to me in the hallway unless I was walking with Monica, it kept me from getting beat up after school every day.

"Can you believe he showed up?" She nods her head towards the guy that Annie was talking about. He has his back to me. From behind, he looks pretty nice. Fit, tall. Broad shoulders. Salt and pepper hair that he's kept cut very short. He's wearing a leather jacket, which is kind of weird given that we're at the beach, but other than that, he definitely looks like kissable material.

Of course, what do I know? I'm currently wound up on wine and adrenaline.

"I couldn't believe it either. Why do you think he came?" At this point I'm just going to play along until I can't anymore.

"You know he always had a big ego. But after that huge break up and then the whole ordeal getting kicked off the football team, I assumed he wasn't friends with anybody here anymore."

He sounds interesting. A big break up *and* getting kicked off the football team? At least he has a story.

The most I can say about my high school experience is that at least I didn't play the flute.

"Some people just have way more courage than others, I guess."

She shrugs her shoulders. "Well, it was good to see you. I almost didn't recognize you! But good for you losing all that weight. I'm going to go get something to eat. See you later!" That explains it. Apparently Emma was rather large in high school, and somehow I passed for her.

"Okay, he's not wearing a wedding ring, and I don't see any women hanging around him. I think he's your best bet. He's pretty good looking."

"I don't know if I can do this."

"Yes, you can. Do it for Aunt Monica. You know if she was here, she would totally do it."

"Don't try to guilt me."

"If you don't kiss this guy, who are you gonna kiss? Some person you see out on the street?"

"How is that any different? This person was just out there on the street. Now he has walked inside of a cafeteria in a high school. He's still the same guy that was just walking out on the street!"

"Mom, you have to do this. Imagine what kind of crazy story this will be to tell people."

I shake my head. "I'm not telling anybody this

story. But, fine. I'll do it. I can't believe I'm going to do this."

"This is so fun!" Annie says, grinning from ear to ear while she claps her hands together. The music is so loud, I hope this guy doesn't hear me coming up behind him. I really don't want him to turn around and punch me before I can kiss him and run.

"You be ready by the door because as soon as I kiss this guy, I'm running straight for you. Have the keys ready, and we're jumping in the car."

"Should I take a video?"

"Why on earth would you take a video?"

"For proof! You have to show the people on the blog."

She may have a point. I can't just say that I kissed a stranger. I have to show proof. "No video. Just take a picture."

"Okay, but you'd better linger long enough so I can click the button."

"You're young. Do it fast. I'm not lingering over some stranger's lips."

With our plan in place, Annie goes and stands by the door. I can see her holding her phone, smiling bigger than I've ever seen. She thinks this is so funny. I don't think this is funny at all. Right now, I imagine myself wringing Monica's neck.

I stay behind the guy, plotting my moves. I don't want to do it in front of a bunch of people, so I wait for him to go off by himself for a moment. He is standing over near the corner where we ate our food. This seems like a good place to pounce. I wait for him to take a sip of his drink, and I run up behind him as quickly as possible, sliding in front of him and pressing my lips to his.

To my surprise, he doesn't pull away. Maybe he's desperate. Maybe he's some kind of pervert.

But I also don't pull away. Warm lips are touching mine, and it's been fifteen years since that happened. I haven't even looked at his face, but I don't want to pull myself away from his lips. And he's not moving. What in the heck is going on?

His hand suddenly touches the side of my neck and then makes it way to the base of my head, pulling me closer. This is weird, but enjoyable enough that I don't want to stop.

After a few moments, I finally pull back, ready to say I'm sorry before running away. But when I look up at his face, my whole body freezes in place. It feels like my feet are stuck to the floor.

"Levi?" The guy from the bar. I just kissed the guy from the bar.

"Jill, right?"

"Why didn't you push me away?"

He chuckles. "Because I'm a guy?"

"I'm so sorry. This was a mistake. I did that for the bucket list thing I told you about."

"Wait, you kissed me for the bucket list?"

At this point he's laughing, and that's ticking me off. Now I kind of want to slap him, but that's not part of the bucket list and would probably be considered assault. I really don't want to go to jail tonight.

"My friend said I had to kiss a stranger, so that's what I just did. I've got to get out of here," I say, looking around for Annie. She was standing by the door, but now I don't see her.

"Did you go to my high school?" He looks down at my name tag. "Emma Eastwick? Wasn't that the girl who was rather large and carried her flute with her all the time?"

"I don't know! I had to crash a high school reunion. How in the world did it end up being your reunion?"

"Lucky, I guess. And, thanks for the kiss. I could feel you enjoyed it."

"You're one of the most infuriating men I've ever met in my life!" I say, turning and heading toward the door. I don't know where Annie went, but she can find me in the parking lot.

"Mom? Where are you?" Annie calls as she walks around the parking lot.

"I'm over here," I call back. I'm leaning against a light pole near our car. Since I didn't have the keys, I couldn't get inside.

"Why did you leave like that?"

"You were supposed to usher me out of there quickly!"

"I had to move over to get a better picture. When I finished taking a few, I looked up, and you were gone."

"I knew him."

Annie's eyes widen. "What?"

"I met him in a bar on New Year's Eve."

"Wait. You went to a bar on New Year's Eve?" She looks absolutely astounded that her mother would go to a bar. "You never told me that."

I roll my eyes. "I don't tell you everything."

"He was kind of cute for an older guy."

I sneer at her. "He's not that much older, and he's not that cute." I walk toward the car.

"Methinks the lady doth…"

"Don't methinks me!" I call back as I walk faster.

"Goodnight, Jilly!" I turn to see Levi standing at the front of the school, waving and smiling. I want to send him a special hand gesture, but the now sober part of me realizes my daughter is watching. Even though she's fully an adult, I don't want to be a bad influence.

Says the woman who just drank too much wine, crashed a high school reunion, and kissed a bar fly.

I don't respond to Levi, with his big toothy grin. Instead, I open the car door which Annie has thankfully unlocked with her key fob, and jump into the passenger seat, leaning my head against the seat. I've never been so excited to get into a car in my life.

Annie gets into the driver's side. "Mom, listen…"

I hold up my hand. "I have a headache. We have a long drive home, and I'd like to take a nap." I turn my head slightly to drive home the point that I don't want to talk right now. I'm grateful when Annie turns on the soft rock station I like and doesn't say another word.

As we head toward home, I can't stop thinking about that kiss. I don't think I've ever had a kiss like that in my life, and that makes me feel guilty. Jesse was a wonderful man, but he didn't kiss me like *that*.

Does everyone kiss like that? Have I been missing
out all these years?

"Wow. That sounds intense." Lila accepted my
invitation to meet up for lunch at my favorite Italian
restaurant. Eating a giant pile of carbs in the middle
of the day probably isn't the best idea, but I don't
have a job right now so I don't care.

"It was intense. I was so embarrassed, though. I
had no idea I knew the guy."

Lila eyes me carefully before taking a bite of her
pasta. "But it sounds like you kind of enjoyed it."

I don't make eye contact. "It's been a long time.
I'd probably enjoy kissing a giraffe at this point."

She laughs loudly, causing two tables full of
people to turn around. "I doubt that would have the
same effect. Listen, it's okay to feel things, Jill. I can't
wait to date again. All the firsts. First date, first time
holding hands, first kiss."

I scrunch my nose. "Sounds terrifying. By the
time men get to our age, they are either divorced,
widowed or never married. Now, the divorced ones
will have baggage, of course, but at least we know
they can commit for some period of time. The

widowed ones scare me because they will always be in love with another woman, and that seems hard to compete with. But, the worst-case scenario are the never-married men. There is definitely something wrong there."

"You think? Maybe they are just very picky and unwilling to settle."

"Oh, that sounds fun to deal with," I say, groaning as I bite into a piece of garlic bread. One day, I'd like to walk around heaven until I find the inventor of bread and thank him or her for such a wonderful contribution to society.

"Love comes in the most surprising ways, you know. Maybe this guy is your soulmate."

I stare at her in disbelief. "He's a cocky, sarcastic - albeit handsome - man. The handsome part is over-ruled by the cocky part."

"You seem awfully fixated on him, though."

I drop my piece of bread and smile slightly. "Lila, that kiss was… I can't even describe it. It was like being lifted out of my body and floating into space. But space was warm and comfy, like a fluffy blanket."

She giggles. "I know about kisses like that."

"Really? I've never experienced anything like that."

"My high school boyfriend. He was a talented guy, for sure."

"Why didn't you marry him?"

She sighs. "His parents didn't approve of me."

"What? Why?"

"His family was quite religious, and my parents got divorced. After that, his mother wouldn't let him date me. I guess she thought divorce was contagious. And maybe she was right because now I'm divorced. Of course, so is he. I saw it on Facebook last week."

"So, reconnect with him!"

She almost spits out her tea. "I just got out of a marriage. I'm not about to jump into the dating scene so soon."

"I have to do the next item on the bucket list soon if I'm going to keep up the pace of finishing everything before Monica's birthday." I still have several more months to do everything, but I just want to get it done.

"So what do you have to do?"

"I don't know yet. I was too afraid to open the envelope. I thought maybe you could help me with that?" I pick up my bag and pull out an envelope, sliding it across the table toward Lila.

"Oh, this is so fun! I love secrets." She quickly

opens the envelope and reads it, her mouth dropping open slightly. That's never a good sign.

"Well, what is it?"

"I have to admit, this would be a tough one, even for me. Let me ask you this - do you get stage fright?"

My eyes widen as big as saucers. "Oh no, is she making me do karaoke? Maybe we can do a duet?"

"It's not karaoke."

"Well, what else could it be?"

"It could be stand-up comedy."

I stop breathing right at that moment. Stand-up comedy? Even professional comedians are terrified when they go on stage to do stand-up. Why on God's green earth would Monica want to do a thing like that?

I swear, she's haunting me. Can people in heaven haunt other people? I'm not really sure how all of that works, but it will be a first on my list of questions for God when I go through the pearly gates. I feel like she's haunting me. It's like Halloween every day.

"Stand-up comedy?" I yell rather loudly. The same two tables turn around and I give them a look. They need to mind their own business no matter how loud we're being. My life is over, and I'm allowed to shout about it.

"That's a tough one. I'll be there for you. I'll sit in the audience and cheer you on."

"I don't know if you've noticed this, but I'm not funny. I might tell a really bad dad joke from time to time, but that's it. There's no way I can get up on a stage in front of a bunch of people and try to be funny. I can't even be funny in my regular life."

"I'll help you practice. Maybe I can help you write some jokes."

"Have you written jokes before?"

"No."

"I've never asked you. What kind of business are you in?"

"I'm an accountant."

I want to lay my face directly in my bowl of fettuccine Alfredo. "I appreciate the offer, but it seems like accountants are some of the least creative people we might have on the planet."

She throws her napkin at me. "Just because I like numbers doesn't mean I'm not creative. In fact, I was in theater and choir throughout high school. Some of us can use both sides of our brain, Jill."

"I'm sorry. I shouldn't have said that. I'm just slightly petrified about going up on stage and having a bunch of people heckle me. They could throw tomatoes or maybe spears."

Lila laughs. "See? You are funny."

"I'm glad you think so. I guess I have to call a local comedy club and get this thing scheduled."

"Let's finish our lunch, and then I'll help you find a place. I know we just met, but I feel like we've been friends forever. Let me help you with this. I need something to take my mind off my own crazy life."

"How are you doing being newly single?"

"I'm okay. My ex-husband is already dating. I think he was dating before we got divorced, actually."

"I'm sorry. I'm sure that's hard."

"Knowing you are so easily replaceable *is* hard."

I realize that I've been totally focused on myself, but Lila has her own issues, too. Everyone does. All these years I've been so focused on my anxiety, which caused me to be more focused on myself than everyone around me. Maybe if I ever get out of that mindset, I'll be able to have more caring and empathy for other people.

Anxiety is a thief. It steals your focus. It steals your fun. It steals your peace. It steals large chunks of your life as you zero in on your symptoms and your thoughts instead of paying attention to everybody around you. For the first time in my life, I'm determined to defeat it. I'm determined to tell it to sit in the back seat while I take us on the rides. Instead of letting anxiety drive, my new goal is to put it in the trunk. It will always be with me, but I need to take back control.

CHAPTER 7

*A*fter lunch, Lila and I walk down the sidewalk, looking into the windows of the local shops. We have a lot more in common than I realized. She's not a big shopper either. I like to get things online so I don't have to deal with running into people at stores. I don't like to be in big crowds, and she feels the same. It's like we were cut from the same cloth.

We get a cup of coffee, and then we sit down and look at my phone to figure out where the closest comedy club is. It's about ten miles outside of town, which is probably a good thing because I don't want anybody I know to see me standing up there, failing miserably at being funny.

I can only assume that Monica is in heaven,

sitting back in her easy chair drinking a big glass of sweet tea and laughing her butt off at me. The thought makes me smile. I have no idea what heaven is like, of course, but I hope to find out someday. Just not too soon. And definitely not while I'm trying to finish this bucket list.

I don't allow myself to think about what it would be like to inherit the money and the house. A part of it makes me feel guilty, like I'm only doing this to get the rewards. And that's partially true. I mean, anybody would be excited about getting a beach house. But more of it is about honoring my friend. Finishing her list, doing the one thing she wanted me to do.

"Okay, they can let you go on next Friday night," Lila says as she presses end on the screen. She's been talking to somebody for the last ten minutes trying to work this out.

"That soon?"

"That gives us over a week to work on some material. You don't have a job right now, so you have all the time in the world. My recommendation is to watch some comedy shows on TV. Go on YouTube, or one of the streaming networks. You should find lots of material there."

"And just take some of their jokes?"

She shakes her head violently. "No! Let's not get you in legal trouble. I mean, watch how they do their delivery. Their timing, their pacing. And maybe it will give you some great ideas for jokes."

"I don't know if I can do this." How many times have I said that in my life? In fact, how many times have I said that just in the last few weeks? I'm realizing that even though I say that, I don't mean it because then I do the thing that I don't think I can do. And each time, I've survived. I have survived zip lining. I have survived the smelly dancing guy. I have even survived kissing a stranger who makes me mad and gives me shivers at the same time.

"You can do this. I know you can. Now, I hate to have to leave you, but I have to meet with one of my clients in fifteen minutes. It's been really fun hanging out with you today. What if I come over tomorrow night, bring some takeout, and we will watch some comedy shows?"

I nod my head. "I've had a good time, too. I'll text you my address."

Lila turns to walk down the sidewalk, looking back to smile and wave before she disappears around the corner. It's so nice to have a new friend. I hope it lasts. And again I feel a bit guilty, like I'm trying to replace Monica so soon. But the truth is, nobody could ever replace Monica. She was a one in a million person, and a one in a million friend.

I STAND in front of Dan's desk, yet again. This is becoming a habit, and just a part of my weekly schedule. He hands me three more envelopes and asks me how the blog is going.

"I think it's going good. So far, people seem to be incredibly entertained by my fear."

He chuckles. "Well, I have to admit I've been reading some of them. You kissed a stranger?"

My face turns all shades of red. I was really hoping nobody would read that one. "Unfortunately, I did."

"That one had me rolling with laughter. You're doing really well with this, Jill. I'm actually proud of you."

"Thanks." Not that what Dan thinks of me means a lot. I barely know the man. But anytime somebody says they're proud of you, you have to say thank you. "I can hardly wait to see what's inside of these envelopes."

"What are you working on now?"

"I have to do stand-up comedy on Friday."

"Oh no. Good Lord. That sounds like an uphill battle. Have you ever done something like that before?"

"I think you know the answer to that."

"Let me take a look here," he says, turning around and scanning his eyes across his giant bookshelf. "Here we go." He takes three books off the shelf and hands them to me. I look down and see that they are books with one-hundred-and-one jokes in each of them. This isn't exactly what I'm going to need for stand-up comedy routine, but I appreciate his thoughtful gesture so I accept them.

"I don't want to take your books."

"Oh, I don't read them anymore. One of my clients gave them to me back in the days when I thought I was going to become a comedian. Then I realized, I'm an attorney. I make a lot of money. Why in the world would I wanna get up on stage and subject myself to ridicule…" He looks completely embarrassed. "I'm sorry. I shouldn't have said that."

"It's fine. Just another one in the long line of things that Monica is doing to embarrass me from her grave."

He laughs. "She really got you good. I wish I had known her in real life."

"I'm blessed to have known her. She was definitely one of a kind."

"Well, my next appointment should be here shortly. See you next week?"

I hold up the stack of envelopes. "It depends on what I find in these. But I'll see you soon, no matter what."

To take my mind off my upcoming demise on stage in front of a bunch of hecklers, I decide to open one envelope and just go do whatever it is. Thankfully, it seems rather benign. Monica wants me to take some kind of class called aerial silks. I'm not even sure what it is until I get on the Internet and look.

Although it isn't something I would pick for myself, it doesn't look too terribly hard. Women climb up these gigantic pieces of silk fabric and move their bodies around in different ways. As long as I don't have to go upside down, I'll be good.

I nervously walk into class, and that's when I realize these women are built like super models and yoga instructors. I'm more what you would call a "really enjoys food" body type. I'm definitely not built for *this*. As I contemplate turning around and going back to my car, I realize I'm just going to end up back here again at some point. I might as well get it over with. I'm certainly not going to let Monica's beach house go just because I don't want to climb up a piece of silk fabric.

After a few minutes of mingling with the other classmates, the instructor steps to the front and introduces herself. Apparently she was in the circus at some point, which makes me think that the only position I might get at the circus is that of a clown or the person who hides in the barrel. Wait, maybe that's a rodeo?

The instructor tells us what to expect, and then she shows it by climbing up onto the silks. That's when I start feeling nauseous, and I worry about that tuna salad sandwich I ate for lunch staying in place. My armpits begin to sweat, and I actually feel my knees knocking together. I wonder if anyone else can hear it?

She directs us each to our own silk cloth, and I walk over to mine, silently begging it to hold me up and not let me fall. Who decided we needed to do this with silk? That seems like the slipperiest of the fabrics. Why not burlap?

As she instructs us, I try to pull myself up onto the fabric, and that's when I realize I have no upper body strength. I have the strength of a sick kitten being fed by a human with one of those little eye droppers, only the kitten is a wee bit stronger than me. I can barely lift myself an inch. As soon as I start to, I get my feet slightly off the ground, lose my grip, and go crashing to the mat below. Thankfully, all the other women are far too focused on their own situation to look at me.

Mortified, the instructor walks over to me to see if she can help. I think I'm beyond help. It's probably not worth her time to even try. I feel a sharp pain in my ankle, but I decide to grin and bear it. I need to be here for long enough to write a blog post about this.

I attempt to shake it off and pull myself back up onto the silk. I make it a little further this time before I slip and fall again. I definitely do not see a future for me in the circus. Or as a stripper.

The class continues, but it's really just like living in a version of groundhog day. I climb, I fall, I hurt another body part. I climb again. One time, amazingly, I get so tangled up that my arms start to ache and I somehow kick my own self in the face. I didn't even know my leg stretched that far. I'm impressed, but definitely expecting to put a bag of frozen peas on my inner thigh later.

Thanks be to God, the class finally ends, and I feel a slight sense of accomplishment. I check another thing off the list, and my confidence is getting a little higher. My ankle hurts, and my face has a big red foot shaped mark on it, but I can't help but smile as I get into the car and make my way home. I will never go back to aerial silks class again, but I will always have the fond memory of overcoming yet one more thing.

ANNIE LAUGHS from the other side of the screen as she reads my latest blog post about the aerial silks class.

"I can't believe you did this," she says, holding up her phone with a picture of me dangling precariously on the silks. Granted, I was only a foot off the ground but the picture my instructor took for me showcases my big behind quite nicely. At least my daughter is getting a kick out of it.

"I'm glad that one is over. More power to those women who can carry their own body weight up a silk cloth or even a metal pole. I'll stay firmly on the ground, thank you very much."

"Are you nervous about Friday?"

"Terrified is more like it. I've been working on my routine with Lila, and she laughs every time I do it. I think she just feels sorry for me."

"I wish I could come! Stupid midterms."

"You focus on school. You have graduation in a few weeks."

"I know, I know. I can't believe Aunt Monica won't be there."

"I wish she could be," I say, holding back tears. Monica raised Annie with me, and she should be there for these big life events. "She'll be there in spirit." That thought always comforts me, and I hope it's true. I hope Monica is watching all of my misadventures and laughing up a storm, just like she would be if she were here in real life.

I miss so many things about her. I miss her loud, cackling laugh that sounded like a cross between a rooster and a drunk hyena. I miss her awful pancakes that were way too thick and way too sweet. I miss her silly dance moves that almost got her arrested for public intoxication outside of a restaurant once. The police officer thought she was drunk, but she was just a terrible dancer.

I miss her calling me Jilly even though I said I hated it. I miss being able to call her at the end of a tough day and have her listen to me. I miss her perfume, even though she always wore too much. I miss her silly socks, her giant hoop earrings that were out of style, and her ability to make me laugh in any situation.

Before I know it, the tears are flowing, and I've forgotten I'm on a video chat with Annie.

"Mom, are you okay?"

I laugh and dab at my eyes. "I'm sorry, honey. I got lost in thought about all the things I miss about Monica."

"Like her inability to sing on key?"

"Yes! Oh my gosh, she was the worst to take on a road trip. I wanted to jump out of the car when we went to Florida last time!"

"Or her horrible smoothie combinations? Who puts sardines in a smoothie?"

I scrunch up my face. "Yes! And she didn't warn me before I drank it!"

We spend a good twenty minutes reminiscing and laughing about everything that was Monica, and at the end it feels like we just celebrated her life in the best way possible.

"You know she'll be there with you on the stage, right?"

"I know."

"And I'll be there cheering you on from afar, too."

"Thanks, sweetie."

"I'm so proud of you, Mom."

"You are?"

"Of course! Despite being scared every step of the way, you've been so courageous honoring Aunt Monica. You're already a different person from when this started."

"You think so?"

"I know so." Annie looks to her left and nods at someone off screen. "I hate to run, but my friends are waiting for me to start study group. I'll call you tomorrow."

"Okay. Love you," I say, but she's already disappeared from the screen. To hear that my kid is proud of me makes me weep even more. It's so rare to hear something like that from your child, and tonight I'm going to savor it.

I AM STANDING BACKSTAGE, staring at the microphone that's in the center of the stage a few feet away. Thankfully, there are a few more people ahead of me in line. But it doesn't matter because my stomach is tied up in knots that even a sailor couldn't untangle. My palms are sweating so much that I fear they will drip on the floor, and my heart is pounding in my chest like a jackhammer. I cannot believe I'm about to do this.

This task definitely sounds like something Monica would've done. And she would've done it fearlessly. She wouldn't have cared what other people thought about her, and she would've laughed her way through it. Instead, I feel like I might vomit.

"How are you doing?" Lila asks. I'm really glad she agreed to come with me because I don't think I could've done this one alone. Why is it so much harder to face the fear of being embarrassed than it is to face the fear of flying through the forest or hanging on a silk fabric?

Even as I stand here, I'm not sure I can do this. I know I keep saying that every time I have a task, but this time feels different. I'm truly terrified that people are going to heckle me or boo me off the stage. It's not like I'm trying to do this for a living or anything, but I still don't want to be mortified and embarrassed.

I suck in a deep breath and blow it out slowly. "Not great."

Lila puts her hands on my shoulders and looks me in the eye. "You're going to do great. You've got some good jokes, and people generally want to see you do well."

"I'm not sure that's true. My experience in life has been that people really like to make fun of other people whenever they can."

"This is a comedy club. People want to laugh. Just remember that when they laugh, that's a good thing."

"Which one of you is Jill?" A big, burly man with an unkempt beard and a giant belly comes walking over. I don't know why he's sweating so bad given that he's not under any bright lights right now. I slowly raise my hand. "You're going on next," he says, before walking away.

I run after him. "Wait! I thought there were a couple more people ahead of me?"

"There were. One of them is throwing up in the bathroom right now, and the other one ran to his car and took off. We get that all the time." Before I can say anything else, he disappears into the dark hallway behind the stage.

"I can't do this!" I say to Lila as I run toward the dressing room. I need to find my purse, and I have to get out of here. Never in my life have I felt so sure of anything. This is not a good idea.

"Jill, calm down! You have to do this."

"No, I don't!" I continue rummaging around in the dressing room. Where did I put my purse?

"Don't you want the beach house? And the money?"

"I'm not a materialistic person. I can live without it," I say, shrugging my shoulders as I finally locate my purse. I strap it across my shoulder, ready to bolt out the door.

"What about Annie?" She just hit my Achilles' heel.

"What is that supposed to mean?"

"Think of what that money can do for Annie. After college, she's going to need some money to start out in life. And think of having grandchildren come to the beach house one day. Playing in the sand, building sandcastles."

I purse my lips and glare at her. "Oh, you're good. A little too good." I toss my purse back into the pile again and walk toward the stage. I can hear the guy in front of me finishing up. He seems to have done a good job because everybody is clapping and laughing. Wait until they hear what I have to say. They'll probably all go to the bathroom at once.

I'm not even sure I'll remember all of my jokes. Even though Lila has gone over that with me dozens of times, my brain feels like a blank slate right now.

Anxiety does that to a person. When you're having a panic attack, your only focus is on the fear. That's what takes center stage. Everything else around you is just a blur, just a side-note to the main event.

The guy ahead of me walks off the stage with applause in the background. He's sweating like he's been running a marathon, and he looks extremely relieved when he walks past me. He doesn't even say anything, but basically runs straight out the door to his car.

I look out at the microphone again, and I swear it's mocking me. The emcee announces my name, and I feel my heart drop all the way to my feet. Suddenly, my mind is a blank. I have no idea what my jokes were, and there's a good chance that I might pass out. Lila squeezes my shoulders one more time and smiles, trying to encourage me, but I can't seem to get my voice to work. Like a zombie, I just start walking toward the microphone.

I step out there as people clap for me. They feel bad for me. They should. I'm about to bomb.

The bright lights over the stage are blinding me, and I can barely see the audience. I can hear them - talking, laughing, drinking. I'm not sure how I can hear them drinking, but I'm well aware that they are.

They wait for me to start, but I just stand there,

frozen in the moment. It's like I can feel the weight of their expectations on my shoulders.

I step closer to the microphone and clear my throat. It makes one of those loud squealing sounds, and people in the front row cover their ears.

"Hi, I'm Jill."

I wait for them to respond, but they just stare at me expectantly. Yes, this is my worst nightmare. This is why most people on the planet would rather actually die than have to do public speaking. Public speaking is one thing, but trying to make people laugh with your words is a different thing altogether.

"Wow, it's bright up here," I say, staring up into the lights. That was dumb. Why don't I just go outside and stare into the sun. Well, for one thing, it's night time, so that's not a possibility. But staring into the lights turns out to be a terrible idea because now the few people I could see in the audience are just giant blue blobs. And I can't tell if the blue blobs are happy or not because they no longer have faces.

"So, who in here has anxiety?"

I have no idea who raises their hands because I can't see anybody. I'm going to assume that the absolute hush over the crowd means that a few of them are raising their hands.

"I've had anxiety my whole life. And I have to tell you, standing up here in front of y'all feels a bit like standing naked in front of the world." I get a few little chuckles, but they are mostly pity laughs.

"Hey, what do you call an anxious dinosaur?" I pause for a moment for dramatic effect. "Nervous Rex." To my surprise, I get a round of laughter. And it's genuine laughter.

"Did anybody else come up that big flight of stairs into the theater? Stairs give me anxiety." Again, I give it a dramatic pause. "That's why I like to take them step-by-step."

This time, people laugh loudly for several seconds. A wave of relief washes over my body. I'm doing this. I'm actually doing this! My hands stop sweating, and my heart rate goes down a bit. I feel my body loosen up as some of my other jokes come back to me.

I spend the next few minutes going through all the jokes that Lila and I came up with. People laugh at every single one of them, and I am so thankful. It renews my confidence in humans. I know I'm not that funny, but these people are cheering me on. When I'm done, I take my bow, and people stand up and clap.

It almost makes me tear up. I know they are

cheering more for the anxious woman who stood in front of them and told jokes. I definitely do not think they are encouraging me to become a professional stand-up comedian.

As I wave at everyone, I walk off stage straight into Lila's waiting arms. She hugs me tightly. As terrible as it sounds, I pretend she's Monica for a moment.

"You did great!"

"Please tell me you got some of that on video for the blog, because I'm never doing that again!"

CHAPTER 8

*a*s the days pass, I get more and more used to doing the bucket list items. Some of them are smaller things that I would've assumed Monica had already done. But I blow through them quickly, such as taking a cooking class and a painting class.

Lila does some of these things with me, and I do some of them on my own. I think part of the reason Monica wanted me to do this was to learn how to do things by myself. I'm getting better and better at it each day.

Today is one of my bigger challenges, and it's not even something that Monica put in one of the envelopes. I know I need to go to her house and start sorting through some things. I know I need to make plans for living there myself. Picking up my life as I know it, as boring as it is, is still quite a hurdle. But even more than that, going into her house again is going to be difficult.

Both Annie and Lila offered to go with me, but I told them this was a thing I need to do alone. Now I'm second-guessing that decision. As I stand in front of her house, the weight of memories is already coming back. I walk up the wooden steps leading to the front door and pull the key out of my pocket. I haven't been to her house since she passed away months ago.

When I open the door, I am overwhelmed by the smell. It's her perfume. It always lingered in the air, and I joked she put on too much. The fact that I can still smell it months later makes me laugh. I feel like she is here with me.

Everything is exactly as she left it. It's both comforting and eerie at the same time.

I push the front door all the way open and walk through the entryway leading to the living room. There's a smell of salt water and sand lingering in the air, and it sets me at ease. It's funny how a scent can bring back so many memories.

I have so many fond memories of spending time with Monica in this home. Lots of laughing, watching movies, eating food we shouldn't have. I try not to think too hard about it because it breaks my heart we won't be making any more memories.

I also think of the times that she wanted me to come visit, and I was too busy. Or I thought I was. Most of the time, it was just because I didn't want to make the long trip in the car. I regret those moments now.

Her living room is bright and airy with walls the color of sand and large windows overlooking the ocean. Sunlight streams in, casting a beautiful glow. The couch is facing the ocean, and there are a couple of armchairs and a bookshelf filled with Monica's favorite books.

I walk over to the shelf and run my fingers over the spines. I remember how she would sit in her chair for hours, lost in a good book. She read over one hundred books a year, maybe more.

I go into the kitchen which is on the smaller side, but cozy. There's a table with two chairs over in the corner, and I notice that Monica's favorite coffee mug is still sitting on the counter. I go over and pick it up, bringing it to my nose. It's clean, but still smells a bit of coffee. I envision her sitting here at the table, looking out over the ocean, having her morning coffee. That feeling soothes me.

I walk into her bedroom, and it looks the same as it always did. A big, fluffy queen-sized bed, her white dresser painted with a custom art design of aquatic life, and her big walk-in closet. There's a window overlooking the ocean, and I sit on the edge of her bed staring at the water coming in and out. I run my hand over her pink and green quilt, trying to hold back my tears. This is where Monica slept, where she dreamed, and where she died. I feel like she's still here and could walk through the door at any moment.

I walk out onto the back deck, which was Monica's favorite spot in the entire house. It overlooks the ocean, and there's a small bistro table with two chairs where she used to sit for hours watching the waves. I stare out over the water feeling so insignificant in the face of the vastness of the ocean.

I reminisce about the memories that Monica and I made in this house. The Fourth of July parties, the lazy afternoons spent drinking tea on the deck. She was so full of life, funny and adventurous. It's hard to believe that energy is gone from the Earth.

As I watch the waves crashing against the shore over and over, I realize that her spirit will always be here. I will see it in little ways like how the sunlight filters through the windows, or the sound of the seagulls, or in the smell of the ocean breeze. I will need to make new memories here, and I think the best way I can honor her memory is by doing just that.

I go back inside the house to her bedroom and open the sliding glass door so I can hear the waves. There's so much to do around here, so many things to sort through. But, for the next little while, I will lie down across Monica's quilt, peppered with her scent, and listen to the roar of the ocean.

TODAY, Dan has offered to meet me at a local coffee shop. I think he's tired of me coming to his office, which is fine by me because it's out of my way.

"White chocolate mocha with caramel drizzle and two pumps of vanilla."

"Wow, Dan. I didn't take you for a froo-froo coffee drinker," I say, needling him.

"Hey, God made sugar for a reason. Who am I to question Him?"

We walk over to one of the tables and sit down while we wait for our drinks. Dan, as usual, is dressed in a Hawaiian shirt and khaki shorts. I'm wondering if he owns any other styles of clothing.

"So, how's business?"

"Always busy. People love to sue each other. How's the bucket list?"

"Not too bad, actually. I almost hate to say it, but I'm having fun."

"Really? That's a plot twist, huh? Boy, I remember the day I had to tell you about this whole thing. You were madder than a wet hen."

I laugh. "I was. I didn't think I was strong enough to do all of this and grieve my best friend at the same time. You know, I went to her beach house earlier this week."

"You finally went? How was it?"

"Emotional, but good. I felt so close to her there. I can't wait to make some new memories."

"I'm glad you're doing so well with this, Jill. I see a genuine change in you."

I smile. "My daughter said the same thing. I don't know if I see it yet."

"Two drinks for Dan?" a young woman calls from behind the counter. He walks over to get them and then hands me my plain latte with light foam.

"No sugar at all?" Dan asks, staring at me like I've grown an extra nose.

"Nope."

"What's the point then?" I hear him say under his breath. "I've brought more envelopes."

"How many more do you have?"

"Oh, just a few."

"Monica's birthday is in a few weeks. I have to keep moving along."

Dan hands me three envelopes. "Here are the next ones."

I decide to open them at the table as my curiosity gets the best of me. "Okay, the first one says plant a flower garden at the beach house and enter a contest. I have no idea why Monica would want to do that. She hated flowers and said they smelled like funeral homes."

Dan laughs. "I can't say I disagree with her there."

"The second one says… volunteer at a shelter for the homeless. I've always wanted to do that. Monica and I even talked about it a few times. I was just too scared to put myself out there."

"Well, now you'll have to."

"And let's see about number three." I open it up and stare at it for a long moment. "What on earth?"

"What is it?"

"She wants me to go on a police ride along."

"That sounds cool!"

"No, it doesn't! Police are in danger all day every day. I don't want to be in danger!"

"I bet it'll be very interesting, Jill."

"Interesting? I can watch one of those cop shows on TV if I want to see police work. I don't need to be in the car, in the line of fire. Is Monica allowed to make me do this?"

He chuckles. "Hon, she's dead, so she doesn't live by any rules at this point."

I put my face in my hands and groan. "I don't like this one, Dan. Not one bit. What if they put me with some weirdo officer? I'll be stuck in the car with this person for hours."

"I think you might be overthinking this one, Jill. Police departments do all kinds of community outreach, including ride alongs. It's not all that uncommon."

"Well, if it's all the same to you, I'll save this little goody for another time. First up, the shelter and the flower garden. I'll work my way up to blood and mayhem."

"Do as you wish. I'd better get going. I have an appointment with my barber. This hair is getting out of control." He swipes at his mane of gray hair and chuckles. He looks a bit like he doesn't own a hairbrush.

As I watch Dan meander down the sidewalk toward his car, I think about the tasks in front of me and wonder if I can do them, especially the police ride along. That is something I've never thought about doing, and I certainly don't want to do it.

I look up and squint my eyes. "Thanks a lot, Mon."

LILA and I stand in the small side yard at Monica's beach house. When I mentioned to her that I was going to have to make a flower garden and enter it in a contest, she got giddy with excitement. It turns out Lila was taught how to garden by her grandmother, who was a notorious green thumb.

I would not call myself a green thumb. Everything I've ever bought in the way of plants has died a slow, painful death. As soon as they are put in my car at the plant store, it's like they're walking to the electric chair. I think the plants know it.

"Okay, so we already have some pre-existing azaleas here, which is good. They will be blooming soon. That will add a wonderful pop of color."

I stare at her. "Whatever you say."

"I suggest we add some other plants. Maybe some

rosebushes, some Gerbera daisies. Oh, and some lantana! How could I forget that?"

"I don't know!" I say, sarcastically, as I throw my hands in the air.

"We might even try some marigolds. I think this is an Encore azalea..." she mutters to herself as I stare out over the ocean. This task is going to be the most boring for me. I've never enjoyed gardening, and I could not care less whether I win a gardening contest or not.

"Are you hungry?"

"I'm always hungry," Lila responds as she bends down and looks at random green sprigs coming up in the garden area.

"What do you say we go inside and make some lunch? I had groceries delivered this morning."

Lila and I drove separately to the beach house because she needs to leave later for an appointment. I'm thankful she agreed to come and look at the garden today so we can start planning for that.

"Sounds good. Have you applied for the contest yet?"

We walk toward the back door to the house. "Not yet. I'm going to do that online today."

As we go inside the house, I'm thankful for air conditioning. Even though it's early spring, it's already getting hot. We don't have long, cold winters in this area. I'm just thankful the humidity hasn't hit yet. Once summer comes, you take a shower, step outside, and you need to take another shower.

"So, I have some big news," Lila says as we walk into the kitchen. I go to the refrigerator and pull out some lunch meats and sliced cheese. I retrieve the bread from the counter, as well as a new jar of mayonnaise. "Oh yeah? What?"

"I'm going on a date this weekend."

"Really? Already?" Lila just got divorced, and I can't imagine going on a date so soon. Especially since she said she wasn't going to date for quite some time.

"I was surprised, too. I really wasn't thinking about dating, but I met this guy at the grocery store the other day. We started talking about cuts of meat, of all things," she says, laughing.

"Are you sure you're ready?"

"Nope," she says, laughing. "But how can we ever be sure we're ready for anything in life? What if this guy is my actual soulmate?"

I roll my eyes. "I don't believe in soulmates." I pour each of us a glass of sweet tea and then push hers across the breakfast bar.

"Sure you do. Otherwise, you would've dated in the last fifteen years, Jill."

"That was grief."

"That was loyalty… and a lot of fear."

"You just met me. You have no idea what the last few years have been like."

She tilts her head slightly. "I'm not judging you. And you're right. I don't know because I wasn't there. But I bet if Monica was here right now, she'd agree with me."

I sigh. "You're probably right about that. She always called me out on my crap."

"Then I consider it an honor to pick up where she left off."

"She's probably clapping in heaven right now."

Lila giggles. "Look, I'm just going to dip my toe in the dating waters. Who knows? I might hate it. I might cry in the middle of the date. I'm willing to try."

"I've recently learned how short life really is, so you know what? I say go for it! I might be too scared to date, but that doesn't mean you have to be."

"Jill, it's your turn."

"What does that mean?"

"You've grieved your husband's death. You've

raised your daughter. It's time to allow love to come into your life again."

I shrug my shoulders. "I'm so out of practice. I barely dated before I got married, and then I was married, and then I was a widow. I wouldn't even know how to meet people these days, much less flirt. I was never great at that."

"Just have fun! You kissed that stranger at the reunion, right? Wasn't that fun?"

I give myself a moment to relive that kiss, and I can't help but smile. "It was pretty dang fun... until I saw who it was."

"But at least you know that you still have those feelings inside you that someone can bring out. You just have to find that someone."

In my mind, I'm mulling over whether that someone could be Levi. The bar guy. No. I'm not falling in love with a guy I met in a bar. He probably travels the area hanging out in bars, hoping for free kisses from desperate women.

Maybe I'll take a note from Lila and find a guy in the grocery store. She's covered the meat department. I'll look in ice cream. He might be a little soft around the middle, but then the competition for him will be less. Very strategic.

We chat for a little while about the garden and

the contest, and I wonder if I have any chance of winning. Lila helps me make a list of plants I need to pick up at the store, and she agrees to come back next weekend to help me put them in the ground. We only have a few weeks before they need to be blooming and beautiful to have a chance to win a contest.

Thankfully, Monica did not insist that I win the contest in order to meet my obligations. She probably knew there was no chance I would ever win a contest related to gardening.

"So, what's next on the list of things you have to do?"

"I'm going to volunteer at the shelter. I actually don't mind that at all. I think it will be very enlightening."

"Do you want me to go with you? I can try to work it around my other appointments."

I smile and shake my head. "For some reason, I feel like this is one of those things I need to do alone. But thanks for offering."

"Okay. If you change your mind, just let me know. I need to hit the road. Send me pictures when you pick up the plants."

"I will."

As I walk her to the front door, Lila turns around

and looks towards the living room again. "I never knew Monica, but I swear I feel her here. I don't know if that makes any sense."

I nod my head. "Monica had a huge spirit. I'm sure many people feel her, but they just don't know what it is. When I first came back here, I had a mix of emotions. Now I just feel comforted every time I walk through the door. I can't wait to live here."

"And I can't wait to visit as often as possible." Lila walks down the front steps and turns around and waves before she gets in her car.

As I close the door, I'm thankful to have a new friend. I know Monica would want that for me. She would want me to live life to the fullest for both of us. She would want me to find love again, and she told me as much many times while she was alive.

The question is, am I brave enough to open my heart to someone again?

CHAPTER 9

I call around to a bunch of places listing themselves as shelters to see if I can come volunteer. Some of them don't allow volunteers to come from the outside, but they will accept monetary donations. Some of them take donations of clothing, toys, and food. Thankfully, I find a few places that will let me come for the day and help in whatever way I can.

The particular place that I find is a shelter for women and children fleeing from domestic violence. This is something I've never had experience with, thankfully. I've had acquaintances in the past who have come out of abusive situations, although I've never talked to anyone about it. I've always been afraid to ask questions and get too personal with people.

As I walk through the front door of the small brick building, a woman greets me with a smile. "You must be Jill?"

"Yes. And you are?"

"Bertha. We're so glad to have you today. It's rare that we get calls from people wanting to volunteer their time, so we appreciate it. I hope you don't mind if we put you to work?"

Bertha has a big personality, and even bigger hair. I don't know if it's real hair or a wig, but I'm a little jealous of how high it sits on top her head. My grandma used to tell me "the higher the hair, the closer to God".

"Please, put me to work." I didn't tell her I was here because my friend left it as an item on a bucket list. That felt disrespectful given the enormity of what these people do every day for the community.

The small brick building is attached to two longer brick buildings on either side. It looks like an older place, possibly a former nursing home or even elementary school. From what I can tell, each of the longer buildings has individual rooms, almost like a motel.

"Well, the first thing I thought we might do is package up some of these gift baskets. We like to give these to the women when they first arrive. They often arrive with nothing because they had to leave it all behind. The baskets have all kinds of essentials in them such as shampoo, soap, razors. Just simple things."

I'm immediately taken aback at the fact that I never thought about how these women show up with nothing. They are literally starting over from scratch. Here I've been going along with my life, being anxious about things like roller coasters and a GPS app, while there are women in the world running for their lives from abusive situations.

I look around the room, and the gravity of this place hits me with full force. The walls are covered with posters giving information on local support groups and other resources. There is also handmade artwork from the children who have passed through these doors over the years. This adds warmth and hope along with a dose of sadness for what they've seen in their young lives.

"I'd be glad to help with that," I say, softly. Bertha sets me up at a table with baskets and a variety of items to put in them. I quietly work on filling them while she fields calls for the next hour. As I listen to her talk with the women on the phone, I'm amazed at her strength and knowledge. I wonder if she's been in their position before, and a part of me believes that to be the case. Of course, I'd never ask her.

As I'm pondering that, a woman opens the door and enters with her two small children. They all look so tired. So frayed. The weight of the world appears to be resting on this woman's shoulders, and her eyes are so puffy and red.

Bertha quietly checks them in, and I try not to make eye contact. I don't want the woman to think I'm staring at her. The heaviness of the emotion in the room is hard to feel, and I can only imagine what situation she's been in before arriving here. It brings tears to my eyes.

As Bertha leads them through a door and down a hallway, out of sight, I stop what I'm doing for a moment and take in a breath. I can't help but reflect on how lucky I am that I've never been through what she's going through. To have never had to flee my home with my kids by my side. To never have had to endure abuse at the hands of a person who was supposed to love me.

Bertha eventually returns and smiles slightly. "You okay there?"

I nod quickly. "Yes. Almost finished."

Her eyes soften as she looks at me. I can tell she gets that this experience is having an impact on me. There is a moment of silent connection between us.

She turns back to her work, and I find myself thinking about the woman and her kids once more. I hope this is the new start she needs, but I will never know.

As I continue filling the gift baskets, I can't help but think about all the women who will receive them. I imagine them as they open the baskets, finding small comforts inside that I take for granted. Hopefully, they also find hope inside them, knowing that a fellow woman packaged them with love and care. That thought brings a smile to my face.

My contribution to this process feels so insignificant in the grand scheme of things, but every little contribution matters. I'm making a difference in my own way, one gift basket at a time.

As I finish my work for the day, Bertha thanks me for my help. It was just a few hours of my life, but it has changed me. I am grateful for the reality check knowing that my problems are often self-inflicted and can be overcome. I know I will come back here soon and volunteer again, not just because I have to, but because I want to.

I STARE AT MY COMPUTER, reading up on all things gardening. I wish I could say I was getting more interested in the topic, but so far that isn't the case. Out of everything I've had to do for this bucket list, the gardening stuff is the most taxing on my brain.

Only a few weeks left until Monica's birthday. I have everything planned so carefully, so as long as I don't get sick or lose a limb, I should finish on time.

I will miss celebrating Monica's birthday with her this year. It's the first one since I was a kid where I won't sit with her while she blows out her candles. I remember one year I thought I was being so sly by getting those candles that you can't blow out. It took her a few tries, but danged if that girl didn't still find a way to blow them out!

The more items I complete on her bucket list, the more I marvel at just how amazing she was. How brave and fearless. She traveled all over the world alone. Not that she didn't invite me. She did. I just wouldn't go. I regret that now. What adventures could we have had if I had just taken a chance?

On the other hand, Monica could never talk me into taking risks while she was alive. Sadly, it took her death to motivate me to change. Have I changed?

Some days I do feel different. Some days I still feel like the same old terrified hermit I was at the beginning.

"Knock, knock!"

I turn to see Lila standing on the other side of my screen door, which I've left open today because spring is turning to summer in South Carolina, and it's getting hot. I'm still not quite ready to turn on my AC and pay the larger bill.

I could stay at the beach house, of course, but it feels wrong to enjoy it full time until I've earned it. I'm weird that way. Even as a kid, I wanted to earn everything. I didn't like when people just gave me stuff. I think there's a feeling of unworthiness under all of this, but I don't like to think about it.

"What are you doing here?" I ask, smiling as I open the door. She's holding a big, brown paper bag.

"I thought we could eat some Chinese food and watch gardening videos. Do you like Mongolian beef?"

I laugh. "How did you know that was my favorite?"

"Good guess," she says as she walks into my condo.

"I'm glad you came. I was about to make a peanut butter and jelly sandwich."

"That's just sad, Jill. You really need to go grocery shopping."

"No, thanks." I hate grocery shopping with a passion. I gave a long speech about it to Lila the other day, in fact. I'm sure she doesn't want to hear it again.

"Did you go by the attorney's office today?"

I nod. "Yep. Got the last stack of tasks. There are more than I thought there were. I have to move faster."

"Have you opened any of them yet?"

"No. I just know about the stupid police ride-along. I'm dreading that."

"Have you called to schedule it yet?"

I don't make eye contact. "Not yet."

"Jill! You know that may take weeks to schedule. You need to get on the phone."

"I'll call them tomorrow."

She points at me. "I'm holding you to that. How many egg rolls do you want?"

I stare at her. "How many do we have?"

Lila chuckles. "You're getting two. Duck sauce?"

"Duh." Sometimes, I forget she hasn't known me all that long. Monica knew I had an affinity for duck sauce. I could eat it with a spoon.

She sits on one of the stools at my breakfast bar. I

have a tiny kitchen, but it serves its purpose. It's not like anybody is usually here with me, anyway.

"Okay, let's open one of those envelopes," she says, her mouth half full with an egg roll.

"I'm eating!"

"Aren't you excited to find out what's next?"

"No. I'm enjoying my peace right now."

"Jill, give me the envelope."

"Fine." I walk over to the table by the front door and retrieve the next envelope in the pile. "Here."

Lila wastes no time and rips it open. Monica always used one of those fancy letter openers. It drove me nuts. I rip my mail open like a wolverine.

"Oh, this one is cool! She wants you to go to a weekend yoga and meditation retreat."

I sigh. "Seriously? That sounds about as boring as watching paint dry."

"I love yoga! I used to go to classes all the time. If you want, I can go with you."

"You know, that might be fun. At least I won't be alone."

"I know a great place. In fact, I have an old friend who teaches yoga at a retreat center about thirty minutes from here. I'll send her a text and see how quickly we can get in."

I have to admit that it's nice to have a new friend.

I'm surprised at how well Lila and I get along. I guess I never expected to find someone else who liked me enough to want to hang out with me. Part of the really poor self-esteem I've had most of my life. Monica always made me feel welcome, and I clung to her for so long. She had lots of friends, and I had her. I guess now I know that I could've had more friends if I had just been open to the possibility.

I've already learned so much about myself during this process. I guess grief does that to a person. It forces you to look inward because you can't look anywhere else.

A few minutes later, Lila's phone dings just as we're finishing up our dinner.

"Is that your friend at the yoga place?"

"Yes. She says we can come this weekend if we want. What do you think?"

"Let's do it. No time to waste!"

She texts her friend and then puts her phone on the kitchen counter. "Are you ready to watch some gardening content?" she asks, laughing. She knows I don't want to do this at all.

"Oh, I can't wait," I say, dryly. Out of all the things I've had to do for Monica's bucket list, this is my least favorite. I enjoy looking at flowers in the springtime, but I'm just not one of those people who wants to get my hands dirty planting them. Once again, I'm thankful that the bucket list item doesn't say I have to win any contests, but just that I have to enter one.

"Come on, it'll be fine. I found a great channel on YouTube that we could watch."

I follow her into the living room, and she turns on the TV. As she searches for the channel, I get myself as comfortable as possible knowing I'm about to have to consume a bunch of information that I don't care a thing about.

I spend the next two hours watching videos. I'm surprised at how much goes into gardening. All of these years, I just assumed people dug holes and stuffed plants in the ground. But there's so much more about fertilizing and planning and insect protection. It's a whole thing. I'm pretty sure once we plant this thing and enter a contest, I will ignore it for the rest of my life.

As we step out of the car and survey the surroundings, I feel a little nervous. Lila, of course, is excited to see her friend and take part in all the yoga and meditation. The retreat is located only about a half hour from my condo, but it's in a sprawling area of forest. It seems like we're out in the middle of nowhere. I've always been more of a suburb kind of gal, so feeling like I'm out in the middle of the wilderness makes me feel slightly uneasy. I'm glad I have someone I know here with me.

We grab our bags and head up to the front desk where we're greeted by a woman with a very warm smile. She looks quite relaxed, and for a moment I wonder if it's really the yoga and meditation, or if she's taking something special to make her seem so serene.

"Hi, I'm Lila, and this is Jill. We're checking in for the weekend yoga and meditation retreat."

I'm thankful that Lila spoke up before I had to. Despite everything I've been doing for the last few months, I still wouldn't consider myself a people person.

"My name is Star. We're happy to have you here. We have a few forms for you to fill out, and then we'll give you the official tour."

She hands both of us clipboards with pens attached to them. We make our way over to the small seating area which consists of a line of beanbag chairs. It's at this point that I wish I was twenty-five pounds lighter because I know getting out of this chair is going to be a bit like watching a turtle try to get up off its back.

After we turn our paperwork in, Star takes us through a door to the left and shows us the yoga studio, the meditation room, and the communal dining area. Through the big windows, she points out several hiking trail options, as well as the direction to go to the lake if we would like to swim or just sit beside it and meditate. It is a calming place. I'll give it that. Besides the ocean, it's probably one of the most beautiful places I've ever seen.

Star shows us to our rooms. Because of the nature of needing to be alone during this kind of retreat, we each have our own separate room. Of course, I'm sure Lila and I are going to hang out together as much as possible.

Lila goes into her room, waving goodbye as she shuts the door behind her. Star walks me to the other end of the hallway and opens the door to room seven. "And this is your room, Jill. You will share the bathroom with the person next-door. I think her name is Willow."

Willow? What kind of name is Willow? Immediately I imagine a skinny woman wearing a long broomstick skirt eating a bag of granola.

"Thanks. I'll just get settled in." The room is

sparsely furnished but has everything I need. There's a bed with white linens, and a large window overlooking the lake.

The first thing I notice is there's no TV. How in the world am I supposed to go to sleep without listening to old eighties TV shows in the background? They soothe me. There's just nothing better than listening to Julia Sugarbaker lull me to a peaceful slumber. Until my bladder wakes me up, of course.

"Everything okay?" Star asks, peeking her head back into the room again.

"Yes, but I noticed there's no TV?" I scrunch my nose up like I've smelled something terrible.

Star smiles. "We don't have TVs here. Our focus is on quieting the mind so we can hear our intuition and soothe our inner child." She continues smiling like some kind of friendly robot, and I consider busting through that nice window and swimming across the lake.

Quieting my mind? Sure, for short periods. But for two whole days?

Soothing my inner child? That just sounds like a bunch of woo-woo stuff I don't want to do. I need TV. TV soothes me.

"No TV? Okay. Not sure how I'll sleep…"

Star chuckles. "No worries. We'll do some yoga and meditation followed by a nice dinner together. You'll be ready for bed by the time we're finished."

Star leaves the room so I can get ready. I stare at the empty wall where a television should be. I still don't think it's cool that nobody's going to let me watch TV while I'm trying to go to sleep. Maybe I'm addicted to TV.

Reluctantly, I change into my yoga clothing, and I walk out into the hallway. Lila is already waiting for me, water bottle in hand. She is way too excited about this.

"Are you pumped about yoga class?"

I stare at her. "Pumped? Is anybody ever pumped about a yoga class?"

She rolls her eyes and laughs. "You're being a stick in the mud. Just think about Monica. You're doing this for her."

I know she's right. It's getting close to dinner-time, and I might be a little hangry. My daughter explained to me that hangry is the result of being hungry and angry at the same time. It's never good to let me get low blood sugar.

As we walk into the yoga room, I'm pleasantly surprised by how serene it is. The lights are dimmed slightly, there are candles lit on multiple tables in the corners. The music is a mixture of flute and river sounds. Star is standing at the front of the room smiling as everyone enters. There are fewer people here than I thought there would be, but that's probably because this was a very expensive retreat.

She instructs us to find a yoga mat. They are rolled out on the floor all over the room. I choose the blue one right next to Lila, who chooses a violet one.

Class starts soon afterward, and we begin with some easier moves. Mountain pose. A forward bend. So far, so good. But as we move along, I quickly realize that I need to do more stretches at home. We get to downward dog, and I'm more like a downward disaster. I'm so stiff, and I can't seem to get in the right position.

Star comes over to me and gently adjusts my pose. She tells me to relax my shoulders and take a deep breath to deepen the stretch, but nothing much happens. My shoulders seem to be permanently attached to my ears.

At that moment, I realize just how stressed I've been for so many years. I'd had no idea what effect it had on my body. I seem incapable of relaxing, and that makes me sad. I realize that Monica sent me on this part of the journey because she knew I needed it. She always knew what I needed. Even when I couldn't see it, she could. How will I live the rest of my life without her?

We do all sorts of poses throughout the class, including tree pose. This is one where you stand up and bring one of your feet to the inside of the opposite knee. It's a balance pose, and I thought I had good balance. And when I fall into Lila and almost knock her over, I realize I do not have good balance after all.

When the class ends, we immediately move into meditation. Star turns the lights down even more, and the music changes to something softer.

This is the part of the evening I have not been looking forward to. I've never been good quieting my mind, not even when I was a little kid. I remember when we used to pray in church, and it was the worst part of the entire service. I loved the music, and I didn't even mind the sermon because our pastor was loud and boisterous. His face would turn red, and I would worry that he was going to have a stroke. He was what one would refer to as a fire and brimstone kind of preacher.

But it was the praying part I didn't enjoy. Not because I don't believe in prayer, but because I didn't like to quiet my mind. Sitting in a room full of people who were quietly praying with their eyes closed made me more anxious. I know, it's weird.

As the meditation begins, my mind races. Did I turn off my stove? Is that a spider on the wall across the room? What am I going to eat for lunch tomorrow? And then that embarrassing moment from sixth grade pops into my mind. And then that thing that boy said to me in eighth grade. Did I pay the light bill?

My mind is all over the place. I realize this is probably what it's like during the day, but I don't notice it because I don't stop to listen. I just let all the crazy voices talk to one another in my head while I maneuver through my day. Is this what I've been saying the whole time? Is this why I'm always so wound up?

I try to focus on my breath, but my brain is like a monkey swinging from one thought to the next. Just when I think I am getting the hang of it, another weird thought comes in. Like, how do I know the color blue is the color blue? I mean, what if I call it blue but other people see something totally different that they consider to be blue? And then I just go round and round with this thought for what seems like an eternity.

Then I hear someone's stomach growling. Is that

my stomach? Is that Lila? How much longer until dinner?

I think of something funny. I don't even remember what it is. I start to laugh, so I stifle it. Then that takes me back to a memory from high school when I laughed so hard that I snorted soda out of my nose. It burned really bad.

The meditation ends, and I'm bummed. Not because it ended. I wanted it to end. I'm bummed because I didn't do well at it. Just another thing that I can't seem to do correctly. I just know if I could somehow quiet my mind, that would be life-changing for me. Oh well, it's dinnertime, so at least there's that.

I make a beeline for the door with Lila right behind me. She's going on and on about how wonderful meditation was. I'm wondering if we were in the same room. We have to walk outside through a breezeway to get to the cafeteria.

"I mean, I don't think I've ever been so calm!" Lila says as we walk into a room with tables and a buffet set up on one wall.

"Well, I'm glad you are. I was off in some other dimension thinking about funny high school memories, and whether I turned off the stove."

168

"Don't worry. I'm sure we're going to do many more meditations before we leave."

I know she means that to be reassuring, but that's not how I'm taking it.

For now, I'm just going to focus on the beautiful assortment of food in front of me. If there's one thing I can do well, it's eat.

CHAPTER 10

*A*fter Lila and I have breakfast, we are instructed to go sit alone in the meditation garden. Lila has her eyes closed and appears to be off in some other dimension. I, on the other hand, am staring at a bumblebee on a flower about six feet away from me. I miss TV.

I feel someone tap me on the shoulder. A turn around to see that it is Star, and she puts her index finger over her mouth. She waves for me to come with her, and I follow her back into the building. She leads me to the meditation room and shuts the door behind us.

"I'm sorry to interrupt your quiet time, but I wanted to talk with you."

"What's going on?"

"It seems that you're struggling here. And if I'm wrong, please tell me."

I shake my head. "No, you're completely right. I don't think yoga and meditation are my things."

"I used to think the same thing," she says, smiling. Star looks like she stepped right out of some commune in the nineteen-sixties. She definitely does not look like anybody who would have struggled with meditation.

"You seem like you are doing pretty well with it."

"Of course, I am now. I know you probably don't believe it, but I used to be a stockbroker."

I almost swallow my tongue. "A stockbroker?"

"Yes. I worked in New York City for three years. If you want high stress, that's the place to go."

"I would've never imagined that you were a stockbroker."

"It was several years ago. But I had what I would consider to be a nervous breakdown, and meditation saved me. So I started studying it, and then I opened this place two years ago. I want to help you because I get the feeling that stress is taking over your life. Am I right?"

"I can't say that you're wrong. I'm only here because my best friend passed away, and I'm trying to finish her bucket list for her. This is one thing she had on her bucket list."

"That's a very noble thing for you to do. But I would like for you to get something out of this. Do you mind if we do a private meditation session right now?"

"I mean, I don't want to take up your time, but I am willing to try."

She smiles. "Good. That's the first step. Being willing to try. Let me get some things set up, and I'll be right back." She stands up and trots off to turn down the lights and turn on some music. She lights some incense. I don't have the heart to tell her I hate incense. "Okay, I want you to take a deep breath very slowly and then blow it out through pursed lips."

At first, I find it incredibly difficult to concentrate on my breath. Again, my mind wanders. I think about the things I need to do when I get home, and I think about the things I've done in the past. I can't seem to shake these feelings of restlessness. But Star continues to be patient, and she reminds me to return to my breath whenever I feel my mind drift.

She instructs me to focus on the sensation of my breath as it moves in and out of my body. She says to notice thoughts that are coming up but don't get caught up in them. She encourages me to be gentle with myself, and to let go of expectations or judgments that I might have about myself or meditation in general.

As we continue, I start to feel my mind clearing. For the first time in all the time I can remember, I can feel what it feels like to be in the present moment. My thoughts are not racing ahead of me. They are staying with me where I am. I feel no worries or anxiety. I'm just here. I want to stay here forever. I feel so liberated, and the stress is lifting. When the session ends, I can feel a smile on my face. I can't seem to wipe it off. It's just there. Star leads me through a visualization exercise where she asks me to envision a place where I'm feeling calm and peaceful.

She tells me to immerse myself in that image. I put myself on the beach behind Monica's house. The warm sand. The blue water. I feel myself standing there so much that I swear I feel the sun on my skin and hear the sound of the waves crashing against the shoreline. I'm grateful for this moment of peace.

A few moments later, Star tells me to open my eyes. I'm still smiling, and I feel some tears running down my cheeks. I had expected the anxiety to immediately return, and I'm sure it will at some point, but right now it's gone. I just feel here, in the moment. I don't think I've ever felt so relaxed.

I thank Star over and over for helping me understand what meditation can really do. And for helping me realize I can do it. She has given me tools I can take home and use.

"This was just a brief session because we have to eat lunch soon, but I'm going to make you an audio recording to take home. That way you can do the visualization exercise with my voice in the background. Would that be helpful?"

Without thinking, I hug her tightly. I don't normally do that. I'm not a touchy-feely kind of person in general. But I'm so grateful to her. This is the first time anyone has ever taken away my anxiety, even for short periods of time.

She looks surprised that I hugged her, but not offended.

"Thank you so much. I have to say that I came here very skeptical. I didn't think this would work for me. But now I believe I can do it. I can help ease my anxiety and get help from meditation. I really appreciate you taking the time with me."

Star smiles. "Every day is a new beginning. We get to choose whether it's a good one or a bad one. It doesn't matter how anxious you've been, or for how long. Today you get to choose whether it's a good day or not so good day. Choose wisely."

As I STAND in the doorway of the local community center, I can't believe my life has been reduced to this. One thing that Monica had put on her list was speed dating. Monica had no problems getting a date, so I can't figure out why in the world she would ever have wanted to do this.

Sadly, it wasn't hard to find a speed dating opportunity. The woman who signed me up assured me there would be interesting men, and I would probably find my dream date there. Highly doubtful but either way, it's something I need to check off my list. I close my eyes for a moment and imagine the waves crashing against the shore behind the beach house. I have to give myself something to look forward to if I'm going to sit down with these guys.

A woman finally walks over and leads me to my table. Apparently, the men are the ones who move from place to place. I sit down and place my hands on the table in front of me. I don't even know what we're supposed to talk about. They gave us a list of all possible conversation topics, but I hate small talk with a passion. This is like small talk on steroids.

Apparently, each man gets eight minutes per table. Eight minutes. Eight whole minutes to figure out if this person could be the love of your life. Or, on the other hand, eight minutes to try to slog through with some guy you can't wait to get rid of.

The woman makes a few announcements and then rings a bell. Suddenly, there's a man sitting in front of me. His name tag says Elliot, and he's wearing a Hawaiian shirt and a wide-brimmed straw hat. He looks to be my age, but he also looks like he needs to move to a retirement village in Florida.

"Hi! I'm Elliot! You're... Jill?" Yeah, dude. That's what it says on this giant name tag I've pasted to one of my breasts.

I nod. "That's me." I've never been very good at hiding my facial expressions. I'm sure this guy can easily tell that I'm not interested in this entire process, but he just continues. Maybe he's one of those people who doesn't take social cues well.

"I'm super pumped about tonight! Are you pumped?"

Am I pumped? I scan my brain and body to see if I'm pumped. Turns out, I am not pumped.

"It'll definitely be interesting," I say, trying to

paste a smile on my face. I probably look like a serial killer right now.

"Well, the paper says to tell each other about ourselves. I'll start. I love pineapple on pizza!" This guy is way too excited about pineapple on pizza. I mean, I can take it or leave it, but it certainly wouldn't be a conversation starter for me.

"Interesting," I say, keeping the smile on my face. My cheeks are starting to hurt.

"Do you like pineapple on pizza?"

"Not particularly."

He looks devastated. That's when I notice there are little pineapples all over his shirt. This guy is dedicated to pineapples. He gets quiet and looks like he'd rather be anywhere else at this point. Probably a pineapple plantation.

"Well, I need to… go to the bathroom."

"What?"

He stands up and looks around. "I have to go to the bathroom. My stomach is hurting."

"Um… okay…" I wonder if he ate too much pineapple before arriving. That will give you a stomachache, for sure.

Without another word, Elliott disappears, and I can't say I'm sad. Now I have a few minutes to gather my thoughts and formulate an escape plan if the next guy is crazy.

"Is everything okay, ma'am?" I turn to see the woman who checked me in at the front desk.

"It's fine. Elliott likes pineapples a lot, and he has a stomachache," I blurt out. She stares at me like I'm the crazy one.

"We still have six minutes left. Let me see if I can find you another partner. I want to make sure you get plenty of chances."

Do I look like I need "plenty of chances"?

"It's fine. Really. I can just wait…"

"Oh! We have a new man who just walked in. Let me grab him!" She runs off behind me, and I wait for the next goofball to sit down across from me. Of course, he might think the same thing about me.

I feel them walking up behind me, and I'm suddenly very aware of what I look like from behind. Tonight, I swept my hair up into a messy bun. Now I'm wondering if it made me look like a bridge troll from behind.

"Jill, this is…"

"Levi?" I say without letting her finish. Why is this guy always everywhere I go?

"Jilly," he says, a satisfied smile on his face.

"Don't call me that."

"Oh, you two already know each other? Wait. Did you already date?"

We both say no at the same time. The woman wanders away, leaving me with this guy I barely know but have kissed. Weird.

"So, how are you?" he asks, still smiling.

"Annoyed."

"Because of me?"

"Maybe," I say, leaning back and crossing my arms like a child.

"We only have five minutes, so let's get to it. Would you rather chat about our lives, or would you rather lunge across the table and kiss me?"

I purse my lips. "I didn't know it was you!" I yell in a whisper.

"Not sure I buy that. You just happened to end up at my high school reunion?"

I stare at him like he's a lunatic. "How would I know where you went to high school? It was pure coincidence."

"Don't you live quite a ways away from Myrtle Beach?"

"Yes, but I purposely chose a place far from home so I *wouldn't* know anyone."

"Right."

"You don't have to believe me. Trust me, if I could

go back and *not* kiss you, I would do it gladly." Lies, all lies.

"Four minutes!" the woman calls over the loud-speaker.

"Why were you in my town if you live in Myrtle Beach?"

"I never said I live in Myrtle Beach."

"Then where do you live?"

He smiles. "I'm not telling you. I don't want you peeking in my window while I'm taking a shower or something."

"Trust me, I wouldn't be tempted." Lies, all lies again.

Why does this guy get under my skin so bad? I'm attracted to him in a way I can't describe, but I also want to smack him across the face just for being alive.

"What do you do for a living?" he suddenly asks.

"Nothing right now." I give in to the small talk because I don't want to keep talking about kissing and showers.

"So how do you support yourself?"

"With my friend's money. Remember the bucket list?"

"Ah, so she left money to complete it? Nice."

"I'd rather have her back and still be working my crappy restaurant job."

His face softens. "I understand."

"Do you?"

He pauses for a moment, then clears this throat. "The night you saw me at the bar, I was wearing a suit because I'd just come from my childhood best friend's funeral."

"I'm so sorry. I had no idea."

"So, I would actually like to apologize if I was a bit of a tool that night. I had more drinks than I normally would, and I was deep in grief. His death was unexpected."

"What happened?"

"He was a cop, and he had an accident on his motorcycle."

"I remember seeing that on the news. I'm really sorry."

"Thanks."

"Two minutes!"

"Why are you here tonight?"

He laughs. "My buddy told me I needed to do something like this. I haven't dated in a long time. Long story. Anyway, he sort of forced me to come. So, here I am."

"And what do you think so far?"

"I think you're stalking me." Thankfully, he smiles after he says it. He has a nice smile. Good teeth.

"I am *not* stalking you. By the way, I have a question."

"What?"

"At the reunion, this girl told me you had some big breakup in high school and got kicked off the football team."

He laughs loudly. "Some people never get over stuff. Yes, I broke up with my high school girlfriend who happened to be the most popular girl in school. Let's just say she was spending too much time with several other members of the football team. Her dad was the coach."

"Ahhh... Well, it was big news to this lady at the reunion. She couldn't believe you were there."

"I guess some people can't stop living in the past."

"Why did you get kicked off the team, though?"

He smiles. "I streaked across the football field when I was supposed to be sitting on the sidelines. He benched me for dumping his daughter, so I showed my... behind... to the whole school. I wasn't very smart back in those days."

"One minute!"

"And just to clarify before we run out of time, I

haven't been stalking you."

"We'll have to agree to disagree," he says, winking at me. He *winked* at me. Why do I feel so flush?

"You're impossible," I say, rolling my eyes. I don't think I've ever done this back-and-forth thing with a guy before. It's like something out of a romantic comedy movie.

"Time's up! Men, please move to your next table."

A part of me feels sad that he's leaving my table. That's weird. I don't even like this guy. He seems pompous and arrogant. And cute. And he likes to wink at me. And I need to talk to my doctor about my hormones or something.

Levi smiles one more time and then walks to the next table which is about ten feet away. I try not to make eye contact with him because I'm supposed to be focusing on the next guy who sits down in front of me. And it's hard not to focus on this next guy because he definitely has a specific look about him. He's wearing a top hat and has a monocle, which immediately puts me on high alert. I never really thought about dating a guy with a monocle.

"Hi, I'm Hector!" He's very animated, with a big toothy grin. I can't tell if he's performing a show, or he knows that he's at a speed dating event. Before I can think much further about it, Hector pulls out a stack of playing cards and starts doing a card trick. I'm trying to pay attention, but his hands are moving so quickly that I can't. Somehow, at the end of the trick, he pulls out a card with my name on it and a heart drawn around it. Yep, now I am creeped out. No doubt about it.

"That was really neat," I say with about as much enthusiasm as somebody who's about to get a pelvic exam.

"I do three shows week down on the strip." And by strip, he's referring to Myrtle Beach where all the shopping and restaurants are.

"That's great. I'm sure you enjoy it."

He beams. "So you like magic?" His accent is so thick that I have to listen to it in my head a second time.

"No, not really. Sorry."

His face drops. "Why does no one like magic?" He shakes his head. I realize he's talking to himself and not really looking for an answer from me. He probably doesn't want to hear my answer.

After the longest eight minutes of my life, another man plops down in front of me. He's wearing a leather motorcycle vest with a patch on it. A skull with snakes wrapped around it. Lovely. Then I notice his beautiful neck tattoo and what seems to be a piece of barbed wire wrapped around his earlobe.

"What's your name?" He says when he sits down. It's not a friendly question. I feel more like I'm about to get interrogated by the secret police.

"Jill. And yours?"

"Rocky." He leans back in his chair, obviously pleased with himself about his name.

"Is that your real name?"

He squints his eyes at me. "It's the name people call me."

"Got it."

As I'm desperately trying to just survive the next few minutes with Rocky, my eyes lock on Levi's. He's sitting at a table with a woman who looks like she probably hasn't been out in a while. He smiles slightly when he sees me look at him. I shouldn't be looking at him. I need to stop running into him.

"So when I got out of prison, I got a job at the motorcycle shop..."

I'm only half paying attention to what Rocky is saying. I heard the word prison, but I'm trying to pretend that I didn't hear that. I'm sure he was only in for something minor like robbery. Definitely not murder. They don't let murderers out, right?

"I have three Pitbulls and two Rottweilers...."

Levi is still looking at me. He looks miserable at his table too. At least he's not afraid of bodily harm from the rather petite woman sitting across from him. He finally goes back to listening to her, and I refocus my attention on surviving my interaction with Rocky.

"Interesting." I know little about what he just said, but I feel like I need to respond in some way. I definitely don't want to irritate this guy.

"Two minutes!"

I've never been so thankful to hear someone yell out two minutes in my entire life. Thankfully, this is the last guy I'm meeting with, and then I can run to my car and get the heck out of here. Silently, I curse Monica in my head. This was one of the worst things I've had to do, even if it's not dangerous. Well, as long as Rocky doesn't follow me to my car, it shouldn't be too dangerous.

"Have you been married?"

"I have. My husband died fifteen years ago."

"Sorry to hear that. I've never been married. I kind of missed those years while I was in prison."

I want to make a joke that you can get married in prison, but I don't think it will go over well so I refrain. After another short amount of time, Rocky has left the table, and I am snatching my purse as quickly as possible. I make my way to the door, and I'm almost to my car when I hear somebody calling out behind me. Please don't be Rocky. Please don't be Rocky.

I turn around to notice that Levi is trotting along behind me.

"I was trying to catch up with you but you're fast!"

"If you had to sit with the last guy I sat with, you'd be getting in your car as quickly as possible, too."

He laughs. "Yeah, he looked like quite a character."

"He was in prison, and I don't want to be the next victim of whatever he did," I whisper. Thankfully, I can see Rocky climbing onto his giant motorcycle across the parking lot.

"You forgot this," he says as he hands me my cell phone. Apparently, in an effort to get out of the building, I had left it behind.

"Thanks. I would be a mess without this thing. Well, I'd better get going."

"It was good to see you again, Jilly."

"I told you to stop calling me Jilly."

He smiles, winks again, and turns to head toward his car. "I know."

CHAPTER 11

*W*hen I offered to meet Lila at the flower garden today to get some work done, I didn't realize just how hot it was going to be. It's not even summer yet! Why in the world is it so hot?

I shouldn't be surprised. The South Carolina Lowcountry is known for heat and humidity, but it's getting an early start this year. Still, we have to get this flower garden planted so that I can put in the paperwork for the contest. I don't know why Lila offers to help me with so many things. I think she's just lonely after her divorce, and sometimes I feel like I'm taking advantage of her by letting her help me.

But Lord knows I need the help. I couldn't do this

alone, and Annie is far too busy finishing up the semester. There are only a few more things on the bucket list, and I don't even know what the last few are. The only one I still know for right now is that I have to do that stupid police ride along.

I put in a call to the police department this morning just to get an idea of what it would involve. They allow ride alongs, but only with certain officers that are trained to do them. Basically, it would be a nighttime ride along, which tells me that there would probably be even more crime going on. It sounds more dangerous.

For now, I'm on my knees in the dirt in a flower garden overlooking the ocean. It's not the worst place I've been, but I certainly don't plan to become a gardener after this. I should've bought one of those little foam pads to put my knees on, but I didn't think about it. So now my knees are turning a very unique shade of brown and it will probably take me days to get it off in the shower.

After only watching YouTube videos and looking at a couple of garden books in the bookstore, I am by no means an expert. Lila seems to have a little more affinity for gardening than I do, but she's also not going to be teaching garden classes anytime soon.

Thankfully, we already have azaleas that were here, and they're starting to bloom. They're actually a beautiful color, kind of a mixture of pink and violet. I'm looking forward to seeing how they do with what we're planting today.

For a moment, I thought about trying to cheat and hiring some landscapers, but I feel like Monica would probably haunt me for that. Somehow, some way I would get caught, and that would be the loophole that kept me from getting the beach house. And I'm really starting to love the beach house.

Every time I come here, it feels more like home. Without Monica, of course, it can't fully feel like home. But I can see myself living here, getting up in the morning with my cup of coffee and sitting on the deck overlooking the water. I can see myself going to bed at night with the sliding door open in the bedroom so I can hear the waves. I can envision myself here, living out memories that Monica didn't get to have.

We're going to be planting some Lantana, Bougainvillea, roses and Gerbera daisies. I know nothing about those, but the books and the videos said they would be good for this area at this time of the year. I was told they are easy to grow, but since I do not have a green thumb, I'm pretty sure it will still be a task for me.

Lila hands me a shovel, and I start digging a hole for the lantana. I don't know exactly how deep it's supposed to be, but I figure deeper must be better. I keep digging and digging until I hit something hard, and sweat is pouring off my forehead.

"What in the world is this?" I stare down into the hole like I'm looking at something I've just discovered.

"I do believe that's a rock, Jill," Lila says, laughing as she looks down into the hole.

"Oh. I guess I didn't think there were rocks near the ocean," I say under my breath. I hear Lila giggle, but she doesn't press the issue any further. I hit the rock a few times with my shovel just to make sure, but eventually confirm that it is, in fact, a rock. I'm able to dig it up and move it out of the way so that my plant can grow in the hole.

We get the lantana planted, and then we move onto the Bougainvillea. It's a little trickier because this is supposed to be trained to go up a trellis. Lila helps me wrestle the trellis into the ground, and then we both stand up and wipe our brows with the backs of our hands.

"Do you think we're making any progress?" Lila asks.

"I think so. I mean we can't do everything in a day. Do you wanna take a break?"

She looks grateful for the suggestion. "I would love that. Why don't we go sit down by the water?"

For a moment, I hesitate. I haven't sat down by the water since Monica passed away, and certainly not with someone else. But, I don't want to seem like some sort of weirdo, so I nod my head in agreement.

We walk down to the water and sit on the sand, looking out over the ocean. I love the smell of the sea air. I love feeling the wind in my face. The thought of living here soon makes me happy in a way I can't describe.

My hands are aching from gardening all morning. It's not the type of activity I'm used to doing. I don't miss working at the restaurant at all, and hopefully I never have to go back. I will have to find something to do for a living even after I move to the beach. Monica has quite a bit in her accounts, but it's not enough to sustain me for the rest of my life.

On top of that, I don't think it's good for me to just sit around and do nothing. I'll just eat all day and never wash my hair, and that doesn't sound like the best course of action for a good life.

"Being down here reminds me of Monica."

Lila looks at me, compassion on her face. "I figured it would. I hesitated to even ask about coming down here, but I think at some point you have to face it."

"Every time I go in the house, I face it. I remember the last time I saw her and had to say goodbye. I thought about getting rid of the bed, but oddly enough, it makes me feel closer to her to sleep in that bed."

"You're so close to living here. Are you excited?"

"I am. I can see a whole new life here. I'm not sure exactly what I'll do for a job, but I feel more hopeful about my future now than I have in a very long time."

"How did the speed date thing go?"

I immediately start laughing. "You wouldn't believe some of the characters I met. A magician did a card trick before he even asked my name. And then there was the biker dude with the neck tattoo and the prison sentence."

"Prison sentence? For what?"

I shrug my shoulders. "I have no idea, and I wasn't about to ask."

"So no possibilities then?"

I don't answer for a moment. Lila can tell I'm

keeping a secret. I don't know why I'm keeping it a secret.

"Well…"

"Well, what?" she asks, bumping her shoulder into mine. "Don't hold out on me!"

"It's just that I ran into that guy again."

"What guy?"

"The one from the bar. And the one that I kissed at the high school reunion."

Lila's mouth drops open, and I fear a seagull might fly in. "Seriously? That's crazy!"

"What's even crazier is that he was only at that bar because his friend passed away, and he had gone to the funeral. He doesn't even live near my house. I think he lives over here somewhere."

"So, was there a spark?"

I wave my hand. "Of course not! We just chatted for a few minutes, and that was that."

"You're totally lying to me. Be honest!"

"What do you want me to say? He's a good kisser, but he's an annoying human being. That's about the long and short of it."

"I think you're attracted to this guy."

"Well, if I am then I have terrible taste. Come on, we need to get back to the garden before we lose our mojo." I immediately stand up and start walking back toward the house, hoping that she will let this go.

"You're not fooling anybody, Jill!" she calls after me. I completely ignore her and walk faster.

ANNIE LOOKS at me from the other end of our video chat. I live for the times that I can talk to her. I know she's busy, and I'm busier now, too. But I really enjoy learning about what's going on in her life. Now that she's an adult, we have a different relationship. I still give her my input, sometimes even when she doesn't ask for it. But we're becoming friends, and that is a gift.

"Are you going to open it?" she urges as I sit there with another envelope in my hand. I'm almost afraid to open it. What if it's worse than the police ride along?

"Yes, I'm going to open it," I say, groaning. I rip open the paper and stare at it for a moment, unsure of why this would've been anything Monica put on her bucket list.

"Well, what does it say?"

"It says to go camping."

Annie's head tilts to the side. "What? Surely, Aunt Monica had been camping before."

Of course she went camping. She hiked the Appalachian trail a few years ago. I doubt she did it without ever sleeping.

"There's no way she never went camping. She went to all of those different countries, she hiked, she backpacked."

"Then why would she leave that for you to do?"

"I have no idea, But it's not like I can ask her. I'm supposed to just do these things."

"Well, it sounds easy enough."

"Are you kidding me? I'm not exactly an outdoorsy kind of gal. I don't like bugs, and bears live in the woods. Like, literally bears with big teeth and giant claws."

"You live near the beach. I don't think there are any bears there, Mom."

"But I can't camp on the beach. I have to go into a forest somewhere. And who am I going to camp with? I can't ask Lila to keep taking time off to be my chaperone at these things."

"Maybe I can go with you after finals."

"I would love that, Annie. And who knows? Maybe it'll be fun. I'll look into tents and see if I can find one with a coffee bar and sauna."

Annie laughs. "You know, you're a lot more relaxed lately. I can see such a change in you, Mom."

"Thanks, honey. That means more than you know."

"So, when's the police ride along?"

I put my face in my hands. "Did you have to ruin our lovely moment? I don't even want to think about that."

"It's that last hurrah before this is all over."

"How do you know? I still have a couple more envelopes to open after the police thing and camping."

"You've gotten over all the big hurdles. I'm sure those things won't be a problem for you. Look how strong and courageous you've become!" Annie holds her arms up and flexes her nonexistent biceps. She's fit and thin, like a ballerina, but definitely not muscular. She got the not being muscular part from me. The fit and thin thing she got from not eating ice cream in her bed… like me.

"Well, we'll cross that bridge when we come to it. For now, I need to call and finalize my ride along date. Ugh."

"You'll be fine. Whoever they match you up with will protect you. Maybe it'll be some hunky cop with arms of steel and a strong jawline."

"You need to stop reading so many romance novels," I say, shaking my head.

"I hate to run, but I have a class in ten minutes. I'll text you later!"

Before I can say another word, she's gone. I lay my phone on the kitchen table in front of me and sigh. I miss my daughter being here every day. Having an adult child is hard. I want her here, but I also want her to fly and build a beautiful life. Maybe I can do the same thing in Pawley's Island.

I pick up my phone and press redial on the number for the police department. No time like the present to schedule this stupid ride along and get it over with. The faster I can finish this bucket list, the better. For the first time in over fifteen years, I'm ready to start my new life.

I'M WALKING along the sidewalk in my favorite shopping area on Pawley's Island. I have a snow cone in one hand and my cell phone in the other. I love lazy days like this. I didn't use to enjoy being alone, but lately I've been kind of digging it.

Before Monica died, I worked all the time. Restaurants pretty much require long hours and exhausting shifts. Now that I don't have to be on my feet all day, I have more time to just enjoy the little things in life.

I stop and look in the window of a hammock store. That's a big thing around here, apparently, and I can see why. Something about being by the ocean makes you want a hammock. No, you *need* a hammock.

I take a seat on a bench to rest my feet for a bit and finish my snow cone. It's Saturday, so I can't help but notice all the families and couples milling about. I see little kids running around, tired and ragged parents chasing them. I remember those days with Annie. My late husband was a good father, and he helped me with her. It was a sweet time in my life.

Sometimes, but not often, I let myself think about one day becoming a grandmother. Annie doesn't even have a steady boyfriend - that I know of anyway - but I assume she'll settle down and have kids one day. I look forward to the day I get to be called grandma by some chubby faced, sticky fingered little kid.

And then a feeling washes over me. I'll be alone. I'll be the grandma with no husband. I rarely let this thought creep in, but now that it's here, it stinks. I hate thinking I might just be alone for the rest of my days.

If that speed dating thing is any indicator of the dating pool in my age range, I'm in trouble. Or maybe I just need to get on board with bad magicians and ex-cons.

I see a couple about my age walking along, hand in hand. I wonder how long they've been married. They're wearing rings, so I assume they are married to each other and not having a rendezvous of some kind.

They stop and eat an ice cream cone as they chat and laugh. The way they look at each other makes me ache with envy. I want that. I didn't even know I wanted it until I started getting out into the world again. Maybe this is what I was afraid of all along - that I would get out of my house and see what was missing from my life. And then I'd have to either live without it or go pursue it.

I feel my eyes welling with tears as I watch this couple I don't even know. I think about how, if all goes well, they'll grow old together and share so many memories. They'll travel. They'll watch their grandchildren grow up. They'll sit on a porch somewhere in their rocking chairs, holding hands until God takes them both home.

Maybe that's a little idealistic, but it feels like I'm missing out on so much. Fifteen years is a long time to spend alone, especially at my age. Have I really been alone since I was thirty-five years old? How is that possible? How have I let that much time pass?

I allow myself to continue wallowing in these ridiculous feelings until my cell phone buzzes in my pocket.

"Hello?"

"Is this Jill?"

"Yes, it is. Who is this?"

"This is Jessica over at the police department. We spoke earlier."

"Oh, yes. Do you have an update on when we can schedule the ride along?"

"Actually, I do. The officer that does those is available tonight."

I sit there, feeling like I've just swallowed my tongue. "Tonight? Isn't that a little soon?"

"Unfortunately, he's going to be out of town for a week, and I know time is of the essence for you."

"Oh. I see." Yes, I do want to get this over with as soon as humanly possible, but the terrified part of me can't imagine doing it tonight. I need time to prepare myself, don't I?

The reality is that the more time I have, the

longer I will worry and fixate on all the things that could go wrong.

"Are you still there?"

"Sorry. Yes, I'm here. What time should I be at the station?"

"At six o'clock. Just tell the front desk clerk that you're doing a ride along with Ace."

"Ace?"

She laughs. "That's what everyone calls him."

Great. A cop named Ace. He sounds like he loves danger and adventure. Just what I need. I contemplate writing out a will, but I have nothing to give Annie except my old purse, and she's made it clear she doesn't want that.

I end the call and continue sitting on the bench, looking at the people milling about with their shopping bags and expensive coffee drinks. I bet none of them are throwing themselves into the abyss tonight, but I am. Thanks a lot, Monica.

CHAPTER 12

J arrive at the station fifteen minutes early. I'm always early, and I don't know why. It just gives me more anxiety to sit somewhere and think about what I'm going to do.

When I go to doctor's appointments, sometimes I arrive thirty minutes early. Then I spend a bunch of time sitting there fixating on what germs are floating around the waiting room or what the doctor is going to say. I imagine all the scary diseases he'll tell me I have. It's a wonderfully productive way of living.

And it doesn't matter what kind of doctor it is. I can get myself worked up at the eye doctor. I once had a panic attack while just trying on frames for new reading glasses. Anxiety is so weird and unpre-dictable.

This whole bucket list thing has helped my anxi-ety, I have to admit. I just don't know if it will last. I'm not super confident yet. After all, I've had almost fifty years to perfect freaking out over nothing. That's not easy to change in just a few months.

"I'm here for the ride along with Ace." His name sticks in my throat for a moment. I imagine this rogue undercover cop who'll be wearing a bomber jacket and those mirrored sunglasses. He'll probably throw me on the back of his motorcycle and drive us straight into a drug deal gone bad.

She nods. "Follow me." This woman definitely isn't winning any Miss Congeniality awards. She seems like she'd rather be in the jail down the road than running the front desk at the police station.

We walk down a long hallway to the back of the building. She opens the door, and I'm in a parking lot full of police cars. "He's over there. You can just get in the passenger side. Better hurry. His shift is starting now."

I hurry down the stairs and open the passenger door. "Sorry. Hope I didn't make you late."

"Seriously?"

In what feels like slow motion, I turn my head

toward the voice I recognize. Levi is sitting behind the wheel, dressed in a police uniform with a bunch of badges and patches. My brain hurts. Have I landed in some alternate universe?

"What are you...? I don't understand..." I can't even form words. I just clutch my purse in front of me and contemplate running away.

"How did you know I work here?"

I stare at him for a long moment. "I didn't know you worked here. I was told I was doing a ride along with some guy named Ace."

"I'm Ace."

I furrow my eyebrows together. "So you lied about your name being Levi?"

"No. My name is Levi."

"Have you been drinking this morning?"

He chuckles. "My real name is Levi. My cop buddies call me Ace. Came from a particularly impressive poker game during my police academy training, and it just stuck."

I groan and put my hand over my face. "I can't believe this."

"So you really didn't know?"

"I really didn't know. This is one of my last bucket list items, and I don't want to do it. Now I really don't want to do it."

"Look, I'm a professional. I won't let anything happen to you."

I realize in my mind that I'm not even scared of the criminals anymore. I'm scared of the guy sitting to my left and how being around him makes me feel. Of course, I would never admit that out loud.

"Let's just go," I mumble, trying to will myself to stay in the car. I need to get this behind me, and I don't want to reschedule at another police department. Also, Levi smells good. He has wonderful taste in cologne. Gosh, I need to talk to my doctor about this hormone situation.

Levi starts driving. "So, the first thing I want to mention is safety. The most important part of this ride along is that you stay safe and stay out of the way."

"Got it. Safety is also the most important thing to me as I do not wish to die tonight."

He looks over at me, his face softer than I've ever seen it. "You're not going to die, Jill. I'm good at my job."

"How long have you been doing this?"

"Twenty-two years."

"Wow. That's a long time."

"But I love what I do. I enjoy protecting my community."

"So, what will I see tonight?"

"You never know. Of course, traffic stops will be a lot of what we do. We'll look for any suspicious activity happening. Hopefully, we won't see any accidents."

"Anything else I need to know?"

"Stay in the car at all times, unless I tell you to get out. If there's an emergency, like I get hurt or become unresponsive, you will need to call for backup."

My mind is spinning. "Unresponsive?"

"It's not likely to happen, but you need to know what to do." He shows me how to use the radio to call for backup. I really, really want to go home now. I know Monica is laughing herself silly right now.

"How long is your shift?"

He smiles. "Until two."

"Lovely," I mutter to myself.

"One of the best parts of being a cop is the community interaction. My goal is to build relationships with the citizens of this community, so we are always courteous and kind."

"Do you really believe that?"

He cuts his eyes at me. "Of course I do. Look, I know cops have a negative perception for some people, and rightfully so in certain cases. But my job is to protect my community and give people a reason to trust us."

Before I can say anything else, he flips on the siren and starts following a small, maroon colored sedan in front of us.

"What happened?"

"Their tag is expired."

The car immediately pulls over, and Levi steps out of the car. I watch him as he walks up to the window, and I wonder how scared he is every time he approaches someone. I've seen terribly scary videos of people pulling a gun, or running over an officer's foot as they speed away.

A few moments later, he returns to the car, looks at the computer, looks at their license and then goes back to talk to them. I can see him smiling and laughing, and he seems to be putting the person at ease. Very different from the time I was pulled over for speeding, and the officer had a Napoleon complex. He was very cocky and rude, and there was no reason for it.

He issues the people a ticket and returns to the car.

"How did that go?"

"About the same as it always does. They weren't happy, but I was able to diffuse the situation."

He starts driving again, and for a while we just sit in silence. Very awkward silence. I don't know what to say to this guy. I'm not sure what to make of him.

"So I'm assuming you live around here?" We are in an area about fifteen minutes away from Monica's beach house. Not quite to Myrtle Beach, but close.

"I do. Just outside of Myrtle Beach."

"What do you think about the tourism?"

He smiles, his dimple appearing. "Hate the traffic, but it sure gives me job security."

I laugh at that. "I bet it does. Are the tourists the ones that are most often getting in trouble?"

"Much of the time. People will come and do things and then claim that they didn't know the laws here. It's not like we're in another country."

There's not much time to get into deep conversation before he pulls someone over for speeding. And then someone for running a stop sign. And then another person for having tint on their windows that is too dark.

Even though these are pretty boring little stops, I'm thankful. I think in my mind I thought we were going straight into battle, and I was going to need a machine gun or something to protect myself. I'm not sure why I thought that because I live out in the world every day, and I rarely see anything criminal going on.

The first couple of hours tick by, and I find myself feeling pretty relaxed. Levi knows what he's doing, and I have to say I do feel protected. Although, nothing really exciting has happened. It's just getting dark, and I assume that when the sun goes down, the craziness starts to happen.

We are also right at the edge of tourism season. People are starting to visit as their kids have gotten out of school for the summer. I'm sure that I'm going to see some interesting stuff as the night progresses.

"Are you hungry?"

"A little. I brought some crackers just in case," I say, pointing to my purse in the floorboard.

"You know, I get a dinner break. We can eat more than crackers," he says, laughing.

"I suppose you do. I never gave it much thought."

"So, where do you like to eat?"

"I'm pretty easy to please when it comes to food, obviously," I say, looking down at my midsection.

He pulls off the road, and I look to see if he's pulling somebody over but I don't see a car in front of us. "Don't do that."

At first, I think I've done something wrong and

broken one of the rules he gave me early on. "Do what?"

"Talk bad about yourself." He's not making eye contact, but looking past me.

"It was just a joke."

"Well, it wasn't a good one. You're a normal-looking woman, and you shouldn't criticize yourself like that."

"Okay, first of all, I was making a joke about food. Second of all, I'm not sure that it's a compliment to call me a normal-looking woman."

"I have to be careful about what I say here. I wouldn't want you to think I'm using my position of authority."

I laugh loudly. Perhaps a little too loudly for the inside of a car. "Your position of authority? Unless you arrest me, I'm pretty sure you aren't in a position of authority."

"So can I say what I want?"

"To an extent."

"You're a very attractive woman, and anyone who tells you otherwise is an idiot." Without saying anything else, he pulls back out onto the road, and I'm left feeling flutters down my spine. It's been a long time since a man said something like that to me.

RACHEL HANNA

A few minutes later, we pull into the parking lot of a diner. I've never been here before, but it looks pretty cool. It has a big retro sign out front, and inside I can see red and white decor with black-and-white checkered floors.

As we go inside, the sound of music overwhelms my senses. There's a real jukebox in the corner, and it's playing fifties music. We walk over to a small booth in the corner, and Levi raises his hand toward one of the servers. She comes over, a big smile on her face.

"Hey, Ace! Good to see ya!"

"Hey, Trish. How are the grandkids?"

"Oh, you know about the same. The teenager is a little wayward, but we're working on him. Do you want your usual?" she asks, pulling out her little pad of paper and a hot pink pen.

"Sure, that sounds good. And this is my friend, Jill."

Trish smiles and cuts her eyes over at Levi. "Your friend, huh?"

He shakes his head. "Well, I wouldn't even say friend just yet. She's doing a ride along with me."

"Oh, that makes more sense," she says, nodding her head. I feel like I'm not even here. I feel like I must be invisible and this woman will never address me directly.

"I'll have a BLT with fries and a sweet tea," I say, handing her the menu. She didn't ask me what I wanted, but I figured I'd move this conversation along. I see Levi giving me an amused look.

"I'll get that ready for y'all," Trish says with her thick southern drawl before she wanders away into the kitchen.

"You must come here a lot?"

"Pretty much every day. They have a great breakfast menu, so when I'm working that shift on the weekends, I'll come here."

"How much longer do you plan to be a cop?"

"I don't know. I wanted to be a police officer since I was a little kid, so I never really thought about doing anything else. I'm not sure what I would do with my time."

"I'm sort of in the same situation. I worked in a restaurant for years, and now I'm going to inherit a beach house and Monica's bank accounts."

He laughs. "What a terrible problem to have."

"I'm just saying that I'll get enough money to survive for a few years, but I still need to have some kind of job or career. I'm turning fifty years old in a few weeks, and I have no idea what I want to do with the rest of my life."

"I don't think you have to be in a hurry about it. What are you good at?"

"Not much of anything. Monica was great at everything, and I was just sort of the quiet sidekick."

He grunts a bit and leans back against the booth. "Why do you do that?"

"Do what?"

"Put yourself down. You do it a lot."

"Oh, like you've been around me enough to know that?"

"Well, you've done it twice in the last hour."

He's probably right. I've always been quite self-deprecating. I think it's a defense mechanism. Say bad things about myself before somebody else can. Say bad things about myself because I assume they're thinking the same thing. I'm not really sure why I do it, but it's just part of my personality now, I guess.

"It's fine."

"It's not fine. I think you're selling yourself short."

"And how would you know that? For all you know, I'm a lazy layabout who doesn't do anything with her time."

"I highly doubt that. You've raised a daughter

who's in college. You've done all this bucket list stuff, mostly by yourself even having high anxiety."

"How do you know I have high anxiety?"

"Again, I've been around you enough to know it."

"I didn't know I was going to get a therapy session with my police ride along," I say, laughing.

"Sorry. I guess I'm just used to trying to get into people's psyches. That's a big part of what we do as officers. We try to get to the truth. We try to get people to tell us things we need to know. I guess I just need to know why you think so little of yourself."

"Look, my husband died fifteen years ago right in front of me. I have beat myself up over and over thinking I could've somehow changed that outcome. My daughter could've had her father, and I could've had my husband. It wasn't a perfect marriage, but it was ours. And I think over the years I've just continued to mentally beat myself up about it. There. Now you don't have to psychoanalyze me while I'm trying to eat my sandwich."

"I'm really sorry about what happened to your husband."

"Thanks."

Trish comes back to the table right at that

moment to give us our drinks. I slurp down my sweet tea hoping we can change the subject.

"So how many more activities do you have to do on the bucket list?"

"Just a couple. I have to enter a gardening contest, which I'm currently working on with my new friend, Lila. We're trying to put together a little garden at the beach house, but it's slow going. Neither one of us are green thumbs."

"I love to garden."

"You do?"

He laughs. "Don't look so surprised. Guys can garden, too. What? Do you live in the dark ages?"

"You just don't strike me as the gardening type."

"Well, you don't exactly know me very well either. You met me briefly in a bar, gave me a long passionate kiss, and now we're riding around town together."

My face turns all shades of red. "I was really hoping you would not bring up the kiss thing."

"How can I not bring up the kiss thing? It's the most exciting thing that's happened to me in a while."

I chuckle. "You're a cop. I highly doubt kissing me was the most exciting thing that has happened to you lately."

"You'd be surprised," he says, softly. This time, Trish interrupts us with food, and I'm a little aggravated. I wanted to hear more about his thoughts on the kiss, but I don't dare bring it up.

We both immediately start eating because he has a very limited dinner break. I don't say another word about the kiss because I'm afraid what road that will take us down, but it is kind of nice to hear him say he enjoyed it. It doesn't really matter, because nothing is going to happen between us, but it's still nice to know I'm at least somewhat attractive to a man.

"I'm going to run to the restroom. I'll be quick." I noticed him looking at his phone over and over to check the time. Thankfully, we haven't gotten any pressing calls on the radio while we've been eating.

I go into the restroom for a few minutes, touch up my face, use the bathroom, wash my hands, and then walk to the door. And that's when I hear it. A lot of loud screaming and shouting. Being an anxious sort, I'm definitely not going to walk toward it. I peak through the little window at the top of the door leading to the hallway of bathrooms. I duck down as much as I can, leaning my head back so that all that can be seen is the tip of my nose and my eyeballs.

I'm shocked when I see a man wearing a ski mask and all black standing in the middle of the restaurant. Everybody has been moved to one side, and he's pointing a gun. My heart pounds in my chest, and I feel like I'm going to throw up the BLT that I just ate. What do I do? I'm careful not to get Levi's attention because I'm afraid he will look over at me and make the robber realize I'm behind him.

I stick my hands in my pockets only to realize I don't have my phone. It's sitting on the table. Now would be a really great time to call 911, even though I'm actually with a police officer. Levi has his hands up as well. Apparently he was taken off guard, and the robber has required him to put his gun on the floor.

He is screaming all sorts of threats, and it becomes immediately obvious that he's mentally unstable. This isn't just a guy who's coming here to get some money. He could really hurt someone. He seems to have a death wish. The more he screams, the more my heart races. I'm getting scared I'll have a heart attack.

It's in that moment that I realize I'm the only chance these people have. This guy doesn't know I'm behind him, and I'm the only one who can possibly get help. I tiptoe to the other end of the little hallway to see if there's a way to the outside but there's nothing. Just two bathrooms and a storage closet. I turn the handle to the storage closet to see if maybe it leads somewhere else, but it's just full of cleaning supplies and random stuff.

Somewhere, deep inside, I feel courage welling up. I don't know where it comes from because I don't think I've ever felt it before. I imagine it would feel something like this if my daughter were trapped under a car and I had to lift it. I would get that surge of adrenaline and be able to lift a car, according to the stories I've read on the Internet. And we all know everything you read on the Internet must be true.

I look around inside of the storage closet to see if there's anything there that could help me. It's mainly just extra napkins, plates, cleaning supplies. There's a broom, but it's about as flimsy as one you would buy at a dollar store. I don't think these people are big on cleaning which makes me second-guess my ingestion of that BLT.

I'm determined to find something in there that can help us, and that's when I see the only thing that makes any sense. For some inexplicable reason, there's a very old timey, heavy-duty vacuum cleaner. This thing weighs about as much as my first car, but thankfully it makes no noise when I'm pushing it. I was afraid it would be squeaky and draw attention to my location. But no noise at all.

I also notice some cleaning sprays. I grab the most potent one of those I can find and make my way back into the hallway. I peer through the window once again, and the man is still screaming and waving his gun around. He still doesn't seem to notice that I'm right behind him.

My hands are shaking, my heart is pounding, and a part of me says to just hide in the closet until this is all over. But as I look around through the little window, I see mothers with children. I see workers just trying to get a bite to eat after a long day. I see a young couple sitting together, holding hands. And I see Levi. Levi who protects the community every single day. I can't just leave him sitting there with no protection.

I say a quick, quiet prayer to God to protect me. I also whisper out loud to my daughter, as if she can hear me somewhere. I want to come out of this alive, and I'm not even sure I'm making the right call here. But somebody has to do something, and I don't even hear any police sirens heading this way. It's entirely possible somebody has called them, and they are on their way, quietly pulling into the parking lot. But I can't take that chance because this guy seems completely unhinged.

I push the vacuum cleaner up to the door. As soon as I open it, I have to run as fast as I've ever run in my life. My plan is to run straight at him, hit him behind his knees, knock him down and spray him in the face with this cleaner. Hopefully, I don't blind him for the rest of his life, but honestly I can't be worried about his health at the moment.

I don't know what's going to happen to the gun in this process. I pray it doesn't go off and hurt somebody. I also pray that he doesn't have a good grip on it, so he drops it and Levi can retrieve it. I'm trying to will all the right things to happen.

I hear him yell something about how he's going to start hurting people. He doesn't even seem to be asking for money. He's just ranting and raving about something that I can't understand. If I'm going to do this, I have to do it now.

I knew I shouldn't have gone on a police ride along!

I wait until he is turned facing completely away from my location, and I run out quicker than I've ever run in my life. Just as I had planned, the vacuum cleaner hits right in the back of the knees, with all its force and metal. It knocks him off his footing, and he falls backwards, almost on top of me. Thankfully, Levi saw me coming, and he has run forward and snatched the gun right out of the man's hand at the same time I spray him in the face. Within seconds, Levi is down on the ground, pinning the man down with his hands behind his back.

CHAPTER 13

*I*t all happened so quickly that I can hardly believe it happened at all. This is not something I would have ever done in my life, or at least I didn't think so. Maybe we all do things in the heat of the moment when they are presented to us.

Moments later, back up arrives, and people are taken out of the restaurant. The robber is put into a car, and diner management decides to close down for the rest of the evening because the staff is so shaken up.

Levi walks over to me as all the hubbub finally dies down. He is staring at me in such an intense way; I feel uncomfortable under his gaze.

"Are you okay?" he asks me.

"I'm fine. I just need this adrenaline rush to wear off," I say, shaking my hands.

Without any other words, he pulls me into a tight embrace. I'm stunned at the show of affection. Slowly he lets go and then steps back a bit, clearing his throat.

"You're crazy. You know that, right? That was an insane thing to do."

"I couldn't just let him hurt people. I was the only one who could do anything."

"Still, you shouldn't have done that. You should've just hidden in that storage room and protected yourself. Do you know what could've happened?"

"But it didn't happen. I'm fine."

He seems beside himself, pacing back-and-forth in front of me. We're standing out in the parking lot now, next to the car. I don't know why we aren't just getting in the car.

"I told you I would protect you."

"You had no gun, and that guy was threatening to hurt people. I was in a position to help, and that's what I did."

"I would've never forgiven myself if something had happened to you," he says, almost so softly that I barely hear him.

"Listen, you protect the public every single day of your life. I only had to be brave for a moment."

I'm leaning against the car now, and he walks forward, leaving very little room between us, one of his hands resting on the car right beside my hip. "I can't do this anymore. I have to take you home."

"But I didn't finish my ride along," I say, complaining about something that I really don't want to do anymore, anyway. I think I've had enough of being a police officer for one night.

"My superior said I can take the rest of the night off. I think we both need to calm down."

The crazy thing is, I feel completely calm except for the extra adrenaline that needs to work its way out of my body. I feel strong and confident for the first time that I can remember in my whole life. I feel like I just did something. I did something Monica would've done. Or maybe Monica wouldn't have even done it.

I did something while I was scared. I did something while I was anxious. I saved lives potentially. I might've blinded a man in the process, but there's always collateral damage when you're a superhero.

I almost start laughing at my own joke. I decide against it.

"Okay, you can just take me back to the station, and I'll drive myself home."

"I don't think so."

"What? My car is at the station."

"I want to see you home."

"Levi, that's unnecessary. I'm perfectly fine."

"I need to take your statement, anyway."

"I think you're making up a bogus excuse. That other officer said I could come down to the station tomorrow and give my statement.

"I outrank him."

I roll my eyes. "Well, I guess my car will be safe at the police station until tomorrow. Fine. You can drive me home."

He opens the door, and I climb inside, unsure of what's going on here. His entire demeanor has changed, and it's making me a little nervous. I'm not scared of him or anything, but I just don't know what to make of it.

He gets into the other side, and we drive in silence for quite a while until he realizes he has no idea where I live. I tell him the address, and he immediately knows where it is. After all, cops are generally pretty good with street names.

About fifteen minutes later, he pulls into the

driveway and under the house. Monica's house is up on those stilts to protect it from hurricanes and flooding.

"Thanks for the ride," I say as I start to step out of the car. He just sits there, staring straight ahead like he wants to say something.

"I lost my wife."

I stop in my tracks and look at him. "What?" For some reason, I just assumed he'd never been married.

"My wife was killed by a drunk driver seven years ago. I showed up on the scene of an accident, and I didn't know…" His voice breaks a little, and that just about breaks me. I don't know what to say.

"I'm so sorry. I cannot imagine how hard it must've been to see something like that."

He stares straight ahead like he's looking into the past. "And when I saw you come running out of that door and engage with that maniac, all I could think was that I was going to watch another woman I cared about get hurt or worse."

The woman he cares about? My brain feels like it's literally spinning around inside my head. Am I hallucinating? Am I having some sort of post-traumatic stress response?

"I don't understand. You care about me?"

"I've cared about you since the moment I met you at that bar. I even went back one time looking to see if you were there."

I laugh. "I did the same thing once."

He looks at me. "You did? I didn't think you liked me at all."

I shrug my shoulders. "I didn't think I did either until I couldn't stop thinking about you after that. You were kind of a jerk for part of that."

"Sorry. I don't do well with funerals."

"Do you want to come in and have a cup of coffee?"

"I'd like that."

We both step out of the car and walk up the front steps, and I feel more nervous now than I did when I was running at the lunatic with the giant vacuum cleaner and the can of cleaning spray. At least I was in control then. Right now, I do not feel in control of my emotions at all.

WE DRINK coffee for a couple of hours, sitting out on the back deck talking about life and listening to the ocean waves. Nothing romantic happens, which is both reassuring and a bummer at the same time. I think I want something to happen, but I'm not sure if I'm ready for something to happen.

He's a perfect gentleman, which is a little surprising. I don't know why, but it is. We decide to watch a movie, and we opt for some old Tom Cruise thing from the eighties. I don't even remember the name of it because I wasn't paying much attention. I couldn't concentrate because I kept smelling his cologne waft across the room to the other end of the sofa.

Before I know it, I'm opening my eyes to the sun shining through the window blinds. I grab my phone from the end table and see that it's seven-thirty in the morning. I turn to look, and Levi is sound asleep, his head leaned back against the back of the sofa, one foot propped up on the coffee table in front of him. He looks so peaceful.

Last night was a revelation to me about the kind of person he is. He talked about his upbringing, his marriage, his police training. He told me about some of his favorite calls, and some of the worst things he'd seen. I still think he was holding back a little, probably not wanting to upset me.

I talked about Annie, about Jesse, and of course, about Monica. We talked about grief, and starting over again.

He had dated a few years after his wife passed away, but he said nothing ever felt right. Nothing ever felt like true love. So he was married to his career, and that had worked well for him.

"Good morning," I hear him say, his voice gruff and gravelly.

"Good morning. I guess we fell asleep before the movie was over."

He chuckles, sitting up straight and running his fingers through his hair. I should probably do the same since I usually look like a bridge troll in the morning.

"I should probably get going. I have some things to do before my shift tonight."

I nod my head. "I can just get an Uber over to the station to get my car."

Everything feels awkward all of a sudden. I don't know exactly what to make of it. Maybe he was just overwhelmed with emotion last night, and a lot of it spewed out. It doesn't mean that he's interested in me in that way.

"I don't mind taking you."

"It's fine. I really wanna get a shower before I go because I have some errands to run after that."

"Okay, if you're sure."

He walks behind the sofa to go toward the door, but his attention is caught by the window leading out to the backyard area.

"Looking at the view one more time?"

He looks at me for a long moment like he wants to say something, but he doesn't. "I was actually looking at your garden. Is that the one for the contest?"

"Yeah. It's a bit of a mess right now."

He chuckles. "It's a lot of a mess, actually. Those two things should not be planted next to each other. This one's going to overpower that one," he says, pointing at things I can't see.

"It's fine. I don't need to win the contest. I just need to enter it."

"A technicality. Anything worth doing is worth doing well," he says, opening the door to the back deck and walking outside.

"I guess we're going outside," I mumble to myself as I follow him.

He stands on the deck overlooking the garden and shakes his head. "I don't know what you were thinking when you planted this. You're going to have a bunch of pink over here, yellow right there, and purple is just going to be over here by itself. Those two things are going to be way too tall, and these things over here don't grow more than a few inches…" He's continuing to ramble on, but all I'm noticing is that little bit of stubble around his jawline that grew overnight. It's very attractive.

"Well, you're welcome to replant it if you'd like," I say, jokingly.

"Seriously? Because I will."

I stare at him for a moment. "So you want to come over to my house, dig up my plants, and replace them?"

"Not exactly. I want to come over to Monica's house, dig up your plants, and replant them."

"Hilarious. It'll be my house soon."

"I'm off tomorrow. I'll go by the plant store, and I'll come by here around mid morning. Sound good?"

"Fine with me. If you want to waste a day doing something like that."

He turns around and smiles at me. "I don't think spending the day with you is a waste of time at all. I'll see you tomorrow, Jilly." Before I can say another word, he walks around the side of the house and disappears, and I feel like I'm going to dissolve into a puddle right next to the rose bushes.

THE NEXT MORNING I wake up with a swarm of butterflies in my stomach. I have no idea what today will bring, and I'm kind of looking forward to it. I make myself a cup of coffee and some scrambled eggs, and I sit at the breakfast table staring out over the ocean. I can only imagine what Monica is thinking right now as she looks down on the situation.

She would have such good advice, probably wrong but good. She would tell me to jump headfirst into this opportunity and see where it goes. She was never one to take things slowly. She was willing to explore any opportunity that came her way, whether it was a relationship, a job, or just some adventurous thing she had never done before.

Every time Levi calls me Jilly, I feel Monica standing close by.

I'm still in my bathrobe when I hear somebody knock at the front door. I wasn't expecting Levi to get here this soon, and he can't see me like this. I'm not one of those women who looks great in the morning like you see on TV. I need makeup. I need a hairbrush. There are things that must be done to make me look presentable to the world.

I run over to the front door and look out the peephole, thankful to see Lila standing there. She's holding a white paper bag, full of pastries no doubt. She has fallen in love with a local bakery and keeps bringing muffins over.

"What are you doing here?" I ask as I open the door. It's not the best way to greet somebody.

She furrows her eyebrows and tilts her head to the side. "What do you mean? We made plans to work on the garden today."

It takes me a moment to recollect that I did, in fact, set a time to work on the garden with her today. Now I'm in a pickle. I'm not sending Lila all the way back home, and I'm definitely not canceling on Levi.

"Of course. Come on in. I'm not good early in the morning." Let's hope she doesn't remember that I used to work a lot of breakfast shifts at the restaurant. I swear, I've told this woman everything about my life. It's a wonder she still comes around.

Lila walks in the kitchen and sets the bag on the counter. She walks over to the coffee pot, and pours herself a cup. It's apparent she's become very comfortable at the beach house, so I think I'll be seeing a lot of her there in the future.

"What's up with you this morning? You're not even dressed."

"We're just working in the garden. Did you expect I was going to put on an evening gown?"

She leans against the counter and crosses her arms. "Is this about that police ride along? How did that go?"

I bite my lip and shake my head. "It was… very surprising." Before I can tell her the crazy story, I need a cup of coffee. More like a bowl of coffee. I pour myself a cup, add all the cream and sugar that will fit, and I go sit at the breakfast table. It won't be long before Levi will come over, so I have to tell her the short version of the story.

"Really? What happened?"

"When I got in the car, it was Levi."

She looks at me for a long moment like she can't process what I'm saying. "Wait. The bar guy? The kiss guy?"

"One and the same."

"He was the police officer? Did he know you were coming?"

I shake my head. "Not at all. They told me I was going to ride with an officer named Ace. It turns out that's his nickname in the police force."

"I kind of dig it."

"Anyway. We went through a bunch of mundane traffic stops, and then it was time for him to have his dinner break. We went to this little diner, and after we ordered I went to the bathroom."

"I hope the story is going to get more interesting soon," Lila says, pretending she's falling asleep.

"When I came out of the bathroom, I heard a bunch of commotion. The bathroom was in this little hallway behind a swinging door with a window. I looked through the window and saw that a masked man was holding everybody at gunpoint. Including Levi."

Her mouth drops open. "What?"

"I'd left my phone on the table, so I had no way to call for help, and there was no exit."

"This is giving me anxiety."

"So I did the only thing I knew to do."

"Which was?"

"I went into the supply closet and grabbed a heavy, old vacuum cleaner and some cleaning spray."

"Because you felt a sudden urge to clean?"

I roll my eyes. "No, silly. I felt a sudden urge to be brave. I ran out of the room, hit the guy in the back of the legs, knocked him to the ground, and sprayed him in the face. That gave Levi time to run over and take his gun."

"You're making this up, right?"

"Why would I make this up?"

"Do you realize how insane that sounds? You, the anxious woman who was terrified to do her friend's bucket list, ran out and attacked a man pointing a gun? With a vacuum cleaner?"

I sit there for a moment and take in her words. I think back to that salsa class and how anxious I was, and now it seems so trivial and silly. Maybe Monica was on to something when she forced me into this crazy scheme.

"I guess it is pretty amazing. Maybe a person can change."

"What I really want to know is what happened with Levi," Lila says, grinning.

"Well… He insisted on bringing me home, so I left my car at the station. We ended up talking all night, watching a movie, and falling asleep on the sofa."

Her eyes get bigger. "Really?"

"Get your mind out of the gutter. It was perfectly chaste. He was a gentleman. I was surprised at how shaken up he was over it."

"Maybe he has feelings for you."

I smile slightly. "Honestly, I think he might."

"And how do you feel?"

"I'm not totally sure. This has been a whirlwind,

the last forty-eight hours. I have something else to tell you."

"What?"

"Levi is coming over today to help with the garden."

"Oh, my gosh! He's totally into you!"

I roll my eyes and walk over to the sink, rinsing out my mug. "You're so dramatic."

"A man does not get up early in the morning to come dig in your garden unless he's interested."

"I need to go get dressed. Can you answer the door if he shows up?"

"Nope," she says, standing up and grabbing her purse.

"Where are you going?"

"I'm not interrupting this love fest. No way."

"You drove over an hour to get here!" At this point, I'm chasing her to the door.

She turns around and looks at me. "He wants to spend time with you, Jill. Let the man have his moment."

"Lila…" As she opens the door, the earth stops turning. On the porch stands a fresh shaven Levi holding two coffee drinks. He's wearing khaki shorts, hiking shoes, and a pale sea foam green golf shirt.

And I'm wearing my ratty white bathrobe, my hair is in a messy bun on top of my head, and there's not a stitch of makeup on my face. There's probably still crust in the corners of my eyes.

Today's headline - "Relationship ends before it starts".

CHAPTER 14

*W*ell, it was good while it lasted. I don't even know if it would've ever turned into anything, but now that he has seen me looking like an ogre, there's very little chance that Levi is going to want to date me.

"Oh my gosh," I say, hiding behind the front door. I stick my hand out so he can still see some part of my body to know I'm there. Maybe I'll do a puppet show for him.

"Good morning," he says, amusement in his voice.

"Hi. I'm Lila." Lila is pretty. Lila is single. Maybe I should just shut the door and let nature take its course.

"Nice to meet you. I didn't mean to interrupt. I

got here a little earlier than expected, but I didn't want the coffee to get cold."

"No, it's fine. Thanks for coming." I'm still hiding behind the door, and I'm pretty sure he thinks I'm crazy now. Well, let's be real, he probably thought that before.

"Hey, Jill? Why are you hiding behind the door?" he asks me.

"I think you know. I wasn't expecting you so soon, and I don't look my best."

"You look fine. Come out."

"No." I can hear Lila laughing.

"So, I'm just thinking it's going to be a little difficult to drink this coffee and work on the garden if you are hiding behind your front door."

"Well, technically it's Monica's front door."

"The coffee is getting cold."

"I like iced coffee, too."

Lila yanks the door away from me. She pulls my arm so that I'm standing front and center again. I might as well just take all my clothes off because I would feel just as exposed.

"Come on in," I say, forcing a smile. Lila giggles down the stairs toward her car. She turns around one more time and waves at me, stifling laughter.

Levi comes inside, and I point toward the kitchen.

"I got you the coffee drink with the most cream and sugar."

"Oh, you know me so well. Listen, I'm just going to go get changed really quickly, and I'll be right back."

Before he can say anything else, I run down the hallway into the bedroom and shut the door. I throw on a pair of shorts, a T-shirt, and slide on the sneakers I've been wearing in the garden. I pull my hair out of the bun, run a brush through it and decide a ponytail is the best way to go. I quickly put on a little makeup with some lip gloss, and I arrive back in the kitchen. The good thing about not being an overly girly girl is that I can get ready in about ten minutes flat.

"I like this outfit, but I thought the robe really added a nice touch," he says, laughing. He's leisurely sitting at the breakfast table, and I flashback to when I was first married. Those early years with Jesse were so wonderful. We'd have breakfast together every morning before he went off to work, and those are some of my fondest memories. Annie and I making a big mess, and me and my new husband sitting there enjoying our morning coffee.

"I didn't want to scare my new neighbors. Well, potential new neighbors."

"You know, you've pretty much done the entire bucket list. This is going to be your house. Why can't you just accept that?"

I sit down across from him and take a sip of my coffee. It's perfect. "I guess it's just really hard for me to believe that I'm going to own a place like this. I could've never bought something like this if I saved my entire life.

"Your friend wanted you to have it. She thought you deserved it, and I do too."

"Thank you. How are you feeling today? About the incident?"

"I'm better. You know, I normally don't let things like that get to me. It's not the first time somebody has pointed a gun at me. I just wasn't expecting to feel how I felt about you being involved."

"I don't know how I feel about it either. I've never done something so crazy and brave. I felt like one of those mothers who lifted a car off her baby."

"Do you ever wonder how those babies get under cars in the first place?"

I laugh so hard I almost spit my coffee across the table. "That's a good question."

"So, are you ready to work on the garden today?

"I am. The judging team is supposed to come out in four days. I still have a lot of work to do."

"We still have a lot of work to do."

"You don't have to help me."

"I do. You might have even saved my life."

"I don't expect to be repaid for that, Levi."

"Okay, then let me just admit that I'm here because I'd like to spend more time with you."

Great. My face is turning red again. That stupid Scottish heritage always gives me away.

"Oh."

"Does that make you feel uncomfortable?"

"No." My brain is yelling yes.

"Listen, I'm not trying to push you into anything. I'm just having a lot of fun getting to know you, and it's been a long time since I could say that about somebody."

"I get it. I feel the same way. It's just a little scary."

He nods. "We'll just take it slow. Who knows what will happen? Maybe we will just end up being great friends."

"Maybe so." A part of me hopes that isn't true. For the first time in many years, I feel something for a man. I want him to want me. This is foreign territory.

"Well, shall we get to it?"

"Definitely. It's only going to get hotter out there as the day goes on."

We spend the next couple of hours puttering around in the garden like an old married couple. It's comfortable yet different. There is no awkwardness though, which was is surprising.

When it finally gets too hot to do anything more, we decide to take a lunch break. The garden is almost done, anyway. Levi is very skilled in that area. It looks beautiful, and I think it will be a genuine contender for the contest.

"I'm sweating like a sinner in church!" I say as we walk into the house. Levi lets out a big laugh.

"I don't think I've heard that one before."

"My grandmother used to say it all the time."

"She must've been quite a character."

I grab two bottles of water out of the refrigerator and slide one over to him. I don't have any food in the house, but I made sure to have plenty of water.

"She was. She actually reminded me a lot of Monica. Always a risk taker. Her husband died when she was young, and she never remarried. She just traveled the world meeting new people and having a good time. I always wanted to grow up to be like her, but as you can see that did not happen."

"You still have time. You're not even fifty years

old yet."

"After my husband died, I never thought I would be single for fifteen years. Maybe I'll be like my grandmother and just be single forever."

"Is that what you want?"

I sit there for a moment and really think about the question. I'm not even sure what I want anymore. This whole bucket list thing has jumbled up my brain in a way I couldn't have expected. I feel like I'm two different people. There's the part of me that's anxious, and then there's a part of me that wants to break free. Currently, they are fighting each other in some kind of cage match.

"No. I don't want that. I didn't realize how lonely I was until my daughter went off to college. The last four years have been the worst. At least when she was home I had something to focus on, somebody to care for. With every passing day, she needs me a little less."

"I can't say I understand that since I've never had kids, but I don't think we should be alone. I don't think we're meant for that."

"Me and you?"

He chuckles. "No. Human beings. I don't think we're solitary creatures."

"I always thought I was fine by myself until I

started going on these adventures and seeing what life really had to offer. I think I was just sort of stuck in my rut and barely living. I still get scared every time I do one of these bucket list items but I feel a little less anxious each time. I think Monica would be really impressed with how I've done."

He smiles. "I think she would too. And I'm glad that you're giving yourself credit for that. So, you said you had a couple of items left? What are they?"

"Well, one is to go camping which sounds just dreadful to me."

"I love camping! Have you ever been?"

"Once as a kid. My grandparents took us, and we stayed in a tent. I got eaten up by mosquitoes, and I had to use the bathroom outside. It was not pleasant."

"Camping is one of my favorite things to do. I wish I had more time for it."

"My daughter says we need to do it up in the mountains. That sounds like a great way to get eaten by a bear to me."

"You just have to follow certain rules if you come across a bear."

"Like don't go camping in the mountains so that you don't come across a bear?"

Levi laughs. "No. If you see a bear, the first thing

you need to do is stay calm and don't make any sudden movements. Definitely don't run away because that might cause the bear to chase you. And believe it or not, they run pretty fast."

"Great. So bears are also track stars. Noted."

"You can also make yourself look bigger by standing up on your tiptoes or raising your arms up above your head."

"You just told me not to make any sudden movements. I think those two statements conflict."

"You want to speak to the bear in a very calm and firm voice. You want to let it know you're human and that you're not a threat."

"So I'm supposed to have a conversation with the bear?"

"No, but you do need to speak up. And then you back away slowly but never turn your back on the bear. You can also bring bear spray with you if you had to use it."

"See, all of that sounds terrifying to me."

"The likelihood of seeing a bear is pretty small. Black bears are generally not even aggressive toward humans unless they feel threatened."

"Before I lose my appetite, why don't we go grab some lunch? I mean, if you have time?"

"I have time. But let's not go to the diner," Levi

says, laughing.

I CAN'T BELIEVE how much I've enjoyed hanging out with Levi these last couple of days. We worked on the garden, had lunch twice, and even met up on one of his breaks for coffee. I'm pretty smitten, and I never thought I would say that about him.

He's actually very smart and funny. When I met him in the bar that night, neither of us was in a good place. Now that I've gotten to know him, I really like him, and that's scary.

Even though I kissed him at the reunion - and what a glorious memory that is - he hasn't made a move at all. Maybe we're in the friend zone already, and I'm just so rusty I don't know it.

Lila says he's interested in me, but I just don't know. I was raised to wait for the man to make a move, but I'm afraid I'll be filling out an application for the nursing home before he makes a move.

"You're going to do what?" Lila is staring at me like I just said I'm going to run for President of the United States.

"I'm going to ask Levi to go camping with me and Annie."

"Are you sure? That doesn't seem like something you would normally do."

I laugh. "You haven't known me all that long."

"So you're saying that you would typically invite a man you have a crush on to go camping with you and your daughter?"

I consider lying about it, but then I fear Monica will have some sort of access to a lightning bolt in heaven and hit me with it. "No, I would've never done that. But it just feels like the right thing to do. I mean, I'm terrified of being out in the wilderness, and Levi is very experienced. And he seemed like he would probably say yes if I asked him."

"That's a pretty big move. Are you sure you're ready?"

"My daughter will be there. It's not like I'm planning to go run off with him and elope. We'll just bring two tents."

"Remember when you used to be too tense?" She waits for a moment and then laughs at her own joke.

"You should never try stand-up comedy." I finish making the sandwich I've been working on for the last few minutes, and then cut it in half, sliding one piece on a paper towel toward Lila. She came to my condo today because there's really no reason to be at the beach house all the time other than that it's a beach house. And it's on the beach. And who wouldn't love that?

"I just don't want you to get your heart broken."

"How will I get my heart broken? He's interested in me. He's told me that."

"I know, but he also seems to have some hangups about what happened to his late wife. How do you know he's even ready to date again?"

"Well, the good thing is I don't have to ask him that because I'm just asking him to go camping with us as a friend and protector."

Even as I say it, I know it's not true. I'm inviting him to go camping because I want to be around him. I want to spend time with him. Maybe I am getting in too deep, but it's been fifteen years. At some point, I have to step out on faith and try to find love again, don't I?

"So when are you leaving?"

"Saturday. I'm meeting up with Levi for lunch tomorrow, so I'm going to ask him. It might be too late for him to even get off of work. I'm not sure what his schedule is. Either way, Annie and I are going out into the woods of the Blue Ridge Mountains on Saturday. We may or may not come back out alive."

Lila laughs. "I wish I could go with you, but I

promised my sister I would help her plan my niece's baby shower."

"It's fine. I'm not overly looking forward to it, especially in the heat, but I'm going to make the best of it."

"You really have become a different person, Jill. I hope you're proud of yourself."

I smile. "I am proud of myself."

WHY DO I feel so incredibly nervous? I spoke to Annie before driving over to meet Levi for lunch. She's perfectly fine with him coming along, but I think that's because she really wants me to fall in love. As a twenty-two-year-old starting her life, I'm sure she wants her old mother to find a life of her own. As it stands, I spend way too much time asking questions about Annie's life than planning a new one for myself. Well, at least until recently.

"Hey! I ordered sweet tea. I hope that's fine?" Levi is sitting at the table of our favorite café. Our favorite. We haven't been out for lunch that many times, but in my head I have labeled it as our favorite.

"Sweet tea is always good," I say, sliding into the

booth across from him and setting my phone on the table.

"I was wondering if you were going to make it."

"Yeah, sorry. Traffic is horrible today." Myrtle Beach during the summer is a tourist mecca, so getting anywhere quickly is practically impossible. That's the only problem with living in a beach town, and I guess it's something I'll have to get used to when I move to Pawley's Island.

"I was surprised that you wanted to meet up for lunch. It's a bit of a drive to get here from your condo."

I smile. "That's because I wanted to talk to you about something…"

"Hey, y'all. What can I get for you today?" the server asks, coming over at the exact wrong moment.

"I'll just have a bowl of potato soup and a cup of chicken salad," I say, handing the menu right back to her. I don't even need to look at it.

"I'll take a cheeseburger and fries." Levi is fit and trim, but somehow he can still put away a cheeseburger and fries without adding any inches to his waistline. Probably related to his job. If I even look at a cheeseburger, I'm guaranteed to gain five pounds.

"I'll be back in a jiffy."

Levi looks back over at me, expectantly. "What did you want to talk to me about?"

"You can tell me if you have no interest in this. I will totally understand. I mean, it is asking a lot, and I don't know what your work schedule is…"

Levi laughs and waves his hands in front of my face. "Since I don't even know what the question is, I have to tell you that your sales pitch really isn't all that great."

"Sorry. I stammer a lot when I'm nervous."

"Jill, you don't have to be nervous around me." He says it in this low, familiar tone that both sets me at ease and gives me chills up my spine.

"Annie and I are leaving for our camping trip on Saturday. We've decided on the Blue Ridge Mountains, so it's going to take us a few hours to get there. Anyway, you seemed so experienced with camping, I just wanted to throw an invitation out for you to go with us. If you want. If you're not busy."

I can see a slight smile starting to cross his face, the edges of his eyes turning up a bit. "Really? You want me to go camping with you?"

"And my daughter." I don't know why I had to make that correction, but it seemed necessary.

"I would love to."

"Wait? You would? It was that easy?"

"I can get somebody to take my shift. That's not a problem. What time do we leave?"

"We were going to leave around six in the morning."

"You'll just have to text me the address of your condo. It makes more sense to leave from there, I'm sure."

"Yes, it will be a little closer. I don't want this to be an inconvenience or get you in trouble at work."

"It won't get me in trouble. And thanks for asking. I was hoping you would."

"You were? Why didn't you just ask me?"

"I was raised to be a southern gentleman, Jill. I don't push myself on women. I figured if you wanted me to come along, you would ask. Now, do you have a tent?"

"I bought this one," I say, holding up my phone and showing him my Amazon orders. He shakes his head.

"That one's not great. It's going to be tiny. I'll just bring two. I'll bring my camping stove and some other necessities. I promise I will try to make this as comfortable as possible for you ladies."

And all I can think in this moment is… swoon.

CHAPTER 15

*A*s we pull up to the campsite on Saturday, I'm exhausted. I've been up since four in the morning packing everything and getting ready. Annie spent the night, so at least she didn't have to drive in so early. She's excited to have this experience with me, but I think she's even more excited to meet Levi. I may have been talking about him a little too much on our calls.

We all rode together, which gave us several hours to chitchat. Levi asked Annie lots of questions about school and her future plans. I could tell that Annie really likes him, and that puts a little more pressure on me.

We get out of the truck, and I'm staring at the campsite. It really is a blank slate. It's flat, and it has a nice view of the mountains off in the distance. Otherwise, there's not much here. I'm suddenly hit with the realization that we're going to have to put up a tent. Two tents actually. And I am not what you would call an outdoorsy woman, so this is all unfamiliar territory to me.

Levi unloads the truck. I try to help, but he swipes me away with his hand. "I can do it."

"I can do it, too," I say, pushing back. I don't know why I'm doing this because I would much rather he unload the truck than to get myself all sweaty. Even though we're up in the mountains and it's cooler than near the ocean, it's still hot. It is June, after all.

"Okay, fine. You take this tent," Levi says, handing me the long, bulky bag. As soon as I pick it up, I almost fall to the ground. It feels like it weighs a thousand pounds.

"Why couldn't Monica just say we needed to stay in a fancy hotel?"

He takes the tent back from me. "I told you I would handle this. Stop trying to be a hero."

I snarl at him playfully and walk off. Annie is already standing on the edge of the campsite, looking at the mountains.

"This is beautiful. I love the ocean, but I've always loved the mountains, too. The air is just so much crisper and cleaner up here." She closes her eyes and takes in a deep breath.

"What do you think of Levi?" I say, chatting with my daughter like we're two middle school girls.

"I think he's great. And I think he likes you a lot."

"You do?"

"Mom, you're out of practice with this dating thing, but that guy has the hots for you big time."

I slap her on the arm. "You're not supposed to say stuff like that to your mother!"

"He's really nice, and he's really respectful. I think you found a good one."

"Well, we'll see how things go."

We spend the next half hour setting up the camp. Levi puts the tents together like he's done it a million times before. They are separated by about ten feet, just to give us some privacy. He will be in his own tent, of course. I think he got the lucky end of that deal. Of course, if a bear comes along, we will all be in his tent while he holds his gun.

Then he sets up a little camping stove and starts a fire.

"Why are we starting a fire when it's four-thousand degrees outside?" I ask.

"Well, we're going to need to cook food later. And

having a fire helps to keep away some of the predators."

"I'd rather not think about the predators. So, what are we going to do to pass the time? It's hours before it gets dark."

"I thought we might go on a little hike?" Levi says. A hike? He expects me to run through the woods looking for the predators?

"Or maybe we just stay here and chat until we can finally go home tomorrow."

"Come on, Jilly. You've become an adventurer, so why stop now?"

I've decided to allow him to call me Jilly. Until Monica died, I didn't realize how much I missed hearing someone say that.

"I wouldn't say I'm an adventurer."

"Why don't you guys go on the hike, and I'll stay here?" Annie says. No way am I leaving my daughter here alone.

"You're not staying here by yourself! Are you crazy?"

"I'll be fine. I've been camping a bunch. If I get scared, I'll just jump in Levi's truck. Nothing is going to get me in there. I'm just really tired, and I don't feel like hiking right now in the heat."

I know what she's doing. She's forcing me to

spend time alone with Levi. She's trying to get me married off as soon as possible.

"I really do think she'll be fine. Here, keep this." He hands Annie the walkie-talkie and clips the other one to his belt. "These work up to five miles. We won't go out very far."

"How are we going to make sure we don't get lost?" I ask, my anxiety creeping up a bit.

He looks me in the eye. "I know what I'm doing. Do you trust me?"

That one question sends me on an entire expedition in my brain. Do I trust him? How do I know I can trust him? I'm going out into the woods with him, so I should know something like that before I leave, shouldn't I?

And then a feeling of peace comes over me. My stomach unclenches. I do trust him. I don't know why, but I do.

"I trust you," I say, softly. Annie is looking at us, a smile on her face. She's already planning my wedding in her mind. I just know it.

A few moments later, we're walking down the pathway to do our hike. I know next to nothing about hiking except that you go out into the woods and try to find your way back. I hear about hikers getting lost all the time, so I sure hope Levi has a good sense of direction.

"Watch your step. There are lots of tree roots around here," Levi directs. "And it is snake season. They can really blend in, so try to make as much noise when you're walking."

"Oh, yes, this is really fun," I say in a deadpan voice.

Levi laughs. "It's going to be fine. I studied this area before we came, so I know exactly where we're going."

"Well, that makes one of us."

"I really like Annie. She's a good kid."

"Thank you. I was very blessed to get a daughter like her. Can I ask you something?"

"Sure."

"Did you ever want children?"

"I did. It just wasn't in the cards for me and my wife. She had some medical issues when she was young, and she had to have a hysterectomy before we even met."

"So you married her even knowing that you would never have children?"

"I did. I wanted kids, but it wasn't something that was going to stop me from marrying a woman I loved."

"That's admirable."

We continue walking, with Levi pointing out all sorts of plants. We watch squirrels running up and down the trees, and we can hear crows cawing overhead. I never realized how loud crows were until I got out into the woods. There's no sound of vehicles. The air is as clean as it gets. We come across several little streams and waterfalls along the way, but when Levi stops at the bottom of the hill and turns us to the right off the path, I hear water louder than I've heard before.

Suddenly, right in front of us is a huge waterfall coming from a couple of stories up, landing in a pool of clear water below. We are the only ones here.

"What do you think?"

"You knew this was here?"

"I told you, I did my research."

I walk closer and lean over to touch my fingers to the water. It's frigid even though it's hot outside.

"I can't believe you found this place. It's spectacular."

"Want to sit on the rocks over there?"

I nod my head and follow him. "I've never seen anything like this."

"Really?" He seems genuinely surprised that at

almost fifty years old, I haven't seen a big waterfall in person.

"I know it seems silly, but I didn't get out much. Monica was always trying to get me to go places and do things, and I was just stuck in my rut. I hope to never be like that again."

"Do you think you'll go back to that?"

"I don't want to. It's just so easy to get stuck that way when you have nothing to look forward to. I spent so many years just existing, and this bucket list thing has forced me to live. Now that I've gotten a taste of it, I would like to continue."

"Yeah, I've been thinking over some things lately. I have a couple of options where my career is concerned, and I'm not sure what to do. I love my job, and I love my community. It's very fulfilling. But there's a part of me that feels like I'm not really living."

I'm surprised to hear him say that. From what I can tell, he lives for his job. But maybe he's a lot like me where he doesn't have anything else to live for on a day-to-day basis. I mean, I have my daughter, of course, but there wasn't much else to look forward to before I started Monica's bucket list.

"What kind of career choices are you trying to

make? I mean, you don't have to tell me if you don't want to."

"I have the option to retire, but I also have the option to take a new job."

"A new job? Where would that be?"

"A few months back, after my friend died, it really made me think about how dangerous my job is. I mostly don't care about stuff like that because it's just me, and I don't have anybody at home waiting for me. But, at the same time, I'd like to live a few more years. A department in Florida is considering me for a job there where I would basically run a new community outreach program. It would give me a fresh start, and I wouldn't be out on the street putting myself in danger."

My stomach clenches into a knot. He might leave? He might move to Florida? Why is my luck always like this?

"So which way are you leaning?" I ask, trying to appear nonchalant.

"I don't know. There's this one factor I didn't consider."

"Oh yeah? What's that?"

There's a moment of silence between us as we look at each other, our faces only about a hand's width apart. I can hear his breath, even over the waterfall.

"Help! Help!" Someone off in the distance is screaming, and we both jump up and run toward the noise.

"Where are you?" Levi calls back.

"Over at the turn. Help!"

We run down the trail a ways before we finally see a man and woman off to the side at the bottom of a cliff area. The woman is standing up, panicking, tears running down her cheeks. The man is laying on the ground, and all I can see is blood on his leg.

"What happened?" Levi asks, immediately kneeling beside the man.

"He was trying to climb up that cliff face. I told him not to do it. He lost his grip and fell down here. His leg is bleeding a lot."

I pull the belt off from around my hiking shorts and immediately kneel next to Levi. "Can't you use this as a tourniquet?"

"Good idea!" Levi says, smiling at me. He looks like a proud parent.

After a few moments, he has the bleeding stopped, and he calls on the radio to Annie who still has cell service. She calls for an ambulance.

As we all wait for help to arrive and Levi tends to

the man, the woman who was screaming earlier sits down, trying to catch her breath. I can see how worried and fearful she is, and I don't blame her. I know she must feel so helpless because I would. I walk over and put my hand on her shoulder.

"Is there anything I can do for you? I have some extra water if you want it."

She shakes her head, tears still running down her face. "No, but thank you. I'm just praying he'll be okay."

"Levi is a police officer, and a good one. He'll make sure he's okay, and help is already on the way. I know he'll be okay."

"Thank you."

"What's your name?"

"Elizabeth. And that's my fiancé, Brian."

"Nice to meet you. I'm Jill."

It takes over half an hour before an ambulance can make its way to the campsite, and then the paramedics can make their way to the hurt man. All of it seems to happen in the blink of an eye. By the time they carry him out of there, Levi and I are exhausted. We go back to sit beside the waterfall before it's time to head back up the trail.

For a while, we just sit quietly, listening to the water. I don't know what Levi is thinking about, but

I'm thinking how life can change so suddenly. One moment, everything is fine, and the next moment you're falling off the face of a rock. Well, that is only if you're crazy enough to climb up the side of a large rock, I guess.

"We make a pretty good team," I say, offhandedly.

"Which brings me back to what I was saying earlier."

"And what was that?" I ask, playing dumb.

"When the opportunity of an early retirement or the job in Florida came about, I only had to think about myself. And maybe that's still the case. But I can't help but consider something else."

"What's that?"

"You."

"Oh, yeah?"

"I can't stop considering you, Jilly. I don't know how you feel about me, but I know how I feel about you."

"You do?"

"Look, when my wife died, I never thought I would feel anything for any woman again. I'm not going to lie. I dated. I went out, and I tried to find someone I cared about. It didn't work, so I gave up. But from the moment I met you, I have felt this connection. Even when you have annoyed me, I still felt a connection."

"I've annoyed you?" I ask, laughing.

"Don't change the subject. I need to know how you feel about me."

My heart is pounding in my chest. I don't think you're supposed to feel your heartbeat in your toes, but I do. Maybe it's my hiking shoes. They are a bit tight.

I want to tell him I think I'm falling for him. I want to say those words. But instead, completely different words come out of my mouth.

"I'm not sure." What on earth? Why did I say that? And then I realize that I don't want to take away his opportunity for a new start if that's what he wants. Maybe he wants to go to Florida. I don't want to be the one that keeps him from doing it. I don't want to be the one that he resents one day.

"Oh."

"I do enjoy spending time with you."

Now there is an awkwardness between us. Before, it felt like we might have a second kiss, and now it feels like he might leave me out in the middle of the woods. I wouldn't blame him. We had this romantic moment going, and I ruined it. I want to believe I did it for an altruistic reason, but a part of me thinks I did it out of fear.

"You know, we should probably head back. I promised Annie that we would make hotdogs." He stands up and turns toward the trail. As we slowly walk back, he says nothing. He looks like he's lost in his thoughts, and I can't blame him. I feel like the world's biggest fool.

As the three of us sit around the campfire that evening, I try to pretend like everything's fine. I think Levi is trying to do the same thing because he's chatting away like nothing ever happened. I'm sure he doesn't want Annie to have a bad time camping. He's considerate that way.

"So you played baseball? Were you good?" Annie asks. Levi has been telling us all about his growing-up years, going to high school, and playing sports.

"I think so. I was the pitcher. I even had some college scouts looking at me for a while, but then I hurt my shoulder, and I sort of missed my opportunity."

"I guess life was meant to take a different path for

you," Annie says, putting her marshmallow back over the fire. She has always been one of those people who liked to burn her marshmallow until it was flaming and then peel off the skin. She does it repeatedly until the marshmallow is so small, it just flops into the fire.

"Yeah, sometimes you just don't know which path life is going to take. You think that one thing is happening, and then something else happens that you weren't expecting."

"Mom, what did you think you would be when you grew up?"

I think for a moment, putting my marshmallow back into the fire again. "When I was really little, I wanted to be a ballerina which was weird because I've never taken ballet."

Levi laughs, and I don't think he means to. I think he's still pretty aggravated at me, but he can't help himself.

"And then when I got into high school, I really wanted to be a marine biologist. But I was too scared."

"Scared of what?" Annie asks.

"Going off to college. Getting in the ocean. Pretty much everything."

"Well, you've overcome a lot of your fears now. I think you've got a really fun future ahead of you."

"Thank you, sweetie."

"Hey, don't you have another envelope to open? Isn't it the last one?"

"Actually, I have two left. I thought there was only one, but they were stuck together."

"Open the next one. Let's see what you have to do."

I walk over to my backpack and pull out the next envelope. The last couple of them were numbered in a specific order for some reason.

When I open it up, I'm shocked to find that it's nothing adventurous at all. It's pretty mundane even though it's something I've never done before.

"It says I have to go stargazing. Surely Monica had done that before. I just don't understand some of these."

"Well, this would be the best place to stargaze. You can't see a thing once you get back into town."

She looks over at Levi like she's giving him a hint.

"She's right. We could drive the truck up to the top of the mountain if you want."

"I'm not leaving Annie here alone."

"Mom, it's just right up there. I'll have the radio. I'll stay in my tent and I'll hold a torch of fire toward any animal that tries to get me."

"If you're sure," I say, looking at her. She smiles and nods her head.

"I'm sure."

Levi gets up and walks over to his tent, rummaging around for something before walking back to the truck. I get in the other side, and we drive up the mountain. It's not a steep drive because we're close to the top, anyway. We can still see the campsite and the fire from where we are.

"You didn't have to do this. I know you're kind of aggravated at me."

He looks over at me. "I'm not aggravated at you, Jill. I'm just confused. But like I've told you before, I'm not going to push myself on anybody." He opens the door to the truck and gets out. I follow.

"Where are we going?"

"Right here." He opens the bed of the truck and pulls a blanket out of his backpack, rolling it out across the cold metal. "Sorry I don't have any pillows."

He helps me up into the bed of the truck, and I sit down on the blanket. He sits down beside me.

"I'm sorry if I upset you."

"Let's just not talk about it anymore. You're supposed to be stargazing." He forces a smile, and then lays back, staring up at the night sky.

I follow, laying down and looking up at the blanket of stars above us. I can't think of a more romantic moment, yet right now I feel completely shattered inside. I have an opportunity in front of me, or rather beside me, and I'm letting it go. I'm sabotaging myself, and for what? There's no reason to let this good man get away just because of a misunderstanding.

"When will you open the other envelope?"

"I guess I could open it anytime."

"How about now?" He pulls a small flashlight out of his pocket and hands it to me. I sit up a bit and pull the envelope out of my pocket, opening it. "Well, what does it say?"

I laugh, a stray tear running down my cheek. "Typical bossy Monica," I say.

"What does it say?"

"It says 'Jilly, fall in love already.'" I lay back against the blanket and wipe stray tears away.

"Oh."

We stare up at the stars for several minutes. I don't think I've ever seen that many stars. I've seen them in the movies, but I always thought that was just some kind of computer-generated image. Now I'm realizing that there are tons of stars in the sky.

I guess I always knew that, but I couldn't see the

stars where I was. I also guess I always knew there were tons of ways to live life, but I couldn't see them. I couldn't see the opportunities I was missing. I couldn't see the joy I was depriving myself of for all those years.

"I don't want you to leave," I suddenly say, looking over at him. He turns his head and looks at me.

"What?"

"I don't want you to leave. I just didn't want to tell you that."

He sits up on his elbow. "Why wouldn't you want to tell me that?"

"I didn't want you to make a choice because of me. I didn't want you to resent me one day for keeping you from that job in Florida."

"Jilly, I was thinking about the job in Florida because I was so sick of living this monotonous existence alone. I didn't want to go. I wanted a reason to stay."

"So? Do you still need a reason to stay?"

Before I can say anything else, he leans in and presses his lips to mine. And just like that, I find my new beginning in the back of a pickup truck, on top of a mountain, under a blanket of stars.

EPILOGUE

One Year Later

I stand on the edge of the platform, looking down into the ravine. Whoever thought bungee jumping was a good idea must have fallen and hit their head. Probably while they were bungee jumping.

"Are you ready?" the young man asks me. No, I'm not ready. Who is ever ready for somebody to push them off of a platform upside down?

"Not quite yet." I say, still staring down into the ravine. I can see Levi over on the bridge across from me, pumping his fist in the air and cheering me on.

For the last year, we've been traveling. We've gone everywhere from Aruba to Germany to Alaska. I've never had such an adventurous year in my life. I now live in the beach house, when I'm home, anyway. I've taken Monica's money and invested it, and I'll also be opening my own coffee shop soon.

Levi retired early so we can travel as much as we want. He said now he has something to live for, and he wants to live to the fullest.

I have flown in airplanes so many times in the last year that I can't even count. That would've been unthinkable to me just a little over a year ago.

Now, I'm getting to do things with the love of my life. Levi is the perfect match for me. He supports me. He challenges me when I need it. He protects me. He's everything I would've ever wanted in a partner, and just seeing him over there pumping his fist in the air is an example of how he supports me in whatever I do.

Of course, when I told him we should bungee jump, he immediately said no. He had no interest. But I would not let this opportunity pass me by. That's such a difference from who I used to be. Now I seek out these moments of excitement. I want these memories that I can live on for the rest of my life.

I think Monica would be impressed with how far I've come. It doesn't mean I'm never anxious. I'm anxious all the time. I just don't let it hold me back from living my life anymore. I even won that stupid gardening contest. Of course, I didn't do it alone. I had lots of help. And wouldn't you know it, those flowers are thriving even now.

When I wrote the last blog post about Monica's bucket list, it was bittersweet because I was closing one of the most important chapters of my life. In a way, I was saying goodbye to my best friend all over again. Her blog readers are still some of my biggest cheerleaders as I continue writing about my own adventures to this day.

Monica also left me her little red sports car. It took me months to get up the courage to drive it. I don't really know why, but every time I ride around Pawley's Island with the top down, wind in my hair, I think of Monica and smile.

The most surprising thing that happened after the bucket list was complete was when Dan handed me one final letter Monica had written to me. In it, she admitted that the bucket list wasn't hers. It was mine all along. She'd been writing it for years, hoping one day to convince me to take a leap and grab hold of life. Those things weren't adventurous to her, but they were to me. She knew just how far to take it because she knew me better than anyone else.

So much has changed in the last year. Even Lila's life is different now. After seeing what happened with me and Levi, she reconnected with her old high school flame, Jack, and they are head over heels in love. Sometimes we even go on double dates.

When Annie told me six months ago that she was moving to California for her new job, I felt sad for myself but so happy for her. That would've broken me a year ago. Knowing that she was going to leave me would have broken my heart. But now I'm able to be happy for her because I'm happy for myself.

"I'm ready," I say, taking another deep breath and blowing it out. I step to the edge, blow a kiss to Levi, and I'm gone. Flying through the air upside down, swinging back-and-forth by my ankles. I can't make heads or tails of anything. But I know I feel alive. I feel crazy. I feel powerful.

Once they get me down, I have to get my footing again. The whole earth feels weird. I make my way back over to Levi who pulls me into a tight hug.

"That looked terrifying!" he says, laughing as he kisses me on top of the head.

"It was exhilarating!"

We are back in our beloved Blue Ridge Mountains for a quick trip before we head to Seattle to do some sightseeing next week. Lila says I keep the roads hot, and I never let grass grow under my feet. I told her those were pretty bad clichés.

It's nice to have a friend like her. Whenever I'm home, we get together and have lunch, lay out on the beach, or gossip. The gossiping is our favorite. I've gotten involved in several things in my new town including a women's networking group. That's how I came up with the idea for opening a coffee shop. It will be a place for people in the community to gather.

"Are you ready for our hike?"

I nod my head. Over the last year, I've lost some weight and gotten into better shape just from getting out and living life again. Now hiking is one of my favorite things to do.

We walk and talk for quite some time until I realize Levi has led me right back to our waterfall. We haven't been here in a year.

I run towards the water, taking off my shoes along the way and putting my feet in. It's so cold, but the air is so hot.

"I've missed this place."

He sits down beside me. "Me too."

"I can't believe how different my life is after one year. I never thought I'd be happy again."

He puts his arm around me, and I set my head on his shoulder. "And you're happy?"

"Of course I am. You know that."

"Where do you see us going next?"

"Seattle, for one," I say, laughing.

"And after that?"

"I was thinking maybe somewhere in Canada."

Levi shakes his head. "That's not what I mean, Jilly. Where do you see our lives going?"

I nuzzle my face into his neck. "I don't care as long as we're together."

He pulls back and stands in front of me. "I feel the same way."

"Good. So do you want to walk over to the waterfall?"

There's this thing about me. Sometimes I can be completely blind as to what's in front of me. I'm off in la la land in my brain, and I don't often pay attention to what's going on around me. That's when I notice he's holding something. A little blue box.

"Jill, I'm trying to ask you a question."

My eyes widen, and my mouth drops open. I slap my hand over my mouth. "What are you doing?"

"I can't kneel or I'll be in the water," he says, laughing. He holds the blue box in front of me and opens it. The most beautiful square-cut diamond ring shines in the light like water dancing. "Jill, you have been the greatest blessing of my life. I can't imagine spending the rest of my life with anyone but you. I want to go on adventures together. I want to support each other. I want to sit on the deck in our rocking chairs overlooking the ocean. Will you marry me?"

I can't see anything now because there are so many tears in my eyes that I feel temporarily blind. I nod my head as quickly as possible and start screaming yes so loudly that people will probably come running. I throw my arms around his neck.

"So that's a yes?" he asks, laughing.

"Yes!"

He puts the ring on my finger, and I hug him tightly. Life really is a series of twists and turns. Some have you going up, some have you going down. Some make you nauseous and sick. Losing Monica was the worst moment of my life, but she knew me. She knew what I needed. She knew I would never do all of this on my own. She didn't need to do any of those things, but she knew I did. And I will forever be grateful for it.

VISIT RACHEL'S store at store. rachelhannaauthor.com.

Made in the USA
Coppell, TX
16 May 2023

16853540R10166